Ghosted Black Ice

By C. Chaney

Part One

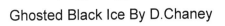

Ghosted Black Ice By D.Chaney

For any writing issues, please contact me below:

*To my bug thank you for being my biggest gift and the only thing that keeps me fighting. I love you baby always . Mark thanks for loving me and my crazy mind. You are the best Mr. Wiggles in the world.*

*To family yea fuck you . You can get a punch in the throat from Kris.*

*Go ahead and flick the pages and get off reading you know you want to.*

*Always check the trigger warning*
*Thank you for being amazing and you are valued on this planet.*

Ghosted Black Ice By D.Chaney

Meet my Nana.

Nana in the story is based on my real life Nana, who was a spitfire.

She will live again through these stories.

Hello, I want to first off and thank you for reading this book, which is part one.

There are going to be issues with the book. This took years to make me struggle with my ADHD and my self-sabotage. There was a lot of self-healing and a decision to add the charter Nana, which is based on my own. Even if I know I read this, I want her to live through books, something she caught on this time here. With all the issues that may come with the writing and issue of this book, I do plan to one day have it edited professionally. For now, a poor girl from Ohio will just have to do the best she can.

I also want to put this here. My books are not for everyone and that is okay because I am not for everyone.

"This one is for all the people who have ADHD and were told they can never work in the smart world. Nana, look what I did all on my own. For now you are my biggest cheerleader from heaven."

Here is a list of what will never happen

Table of contents

Ghosted Black Ice By D.Chaney

Chapter One - Drive thru stop

Emma

"Get home ladies and gentlemen, the blizzard has arrived and is hitting Ohio. If you happen to be out, take it slow and steady, and don't panic."

The radio man has been warning all the Ohio residents of the blizzard that's about to hit. I know I should be home, I just had to make a stop before I could rest.

Pulling up to the light, I see my location:: the family drive-thru on the left. The lights are on, and the place is in full function. The drive-thru would be open no matter what.

Pulling in front of one of the two doors facing me. One led to the apartment upstairs. That creepy place, if it's not haunted I would be shocked as hell by the amount of fires that apartment has had. The other door leads to pick-up if you do want to go through the drive-through. Getting out of the car and shutting the door I flip my hood up and take a few steps back. The sign in big letters was like a beacon.

Nana's drive-thru beer, wine, pizza, and subs I spent many hours in this place growing up. I know everything there is about this place. My heart and soul feel at peace and calm here. I was about to go to battle with the most stubborn ass person and I will need this old place to keep me in check.

Steadying myself and trying not to let the cold air hit my face I make that walk to the first door. Gripping the handle I look inside and see Nana, yes my Nana moving around the place pulling pizzas from the oven putting them in pizza boxes. I hear the phone ringing on the wall. I know I look like a creeper standing here looking through the window but anyone who takes a look at me knows me and everyone in the area knows me and my car. I watch

Nana walk over and pick up the phone order pad in hand.

Pulling the door open the heat from the fryers and oven hit me in the face the smell of pizza and the deep fryer. Stepping in Nana already knows I am there, the bell above the door alerted her of my entrance.

In front of me are a few orders on the counter with names. The old cash register is in the center of the counter underneath glass windows to show candies. Penny gummy candy alongside the candy bars. Making sure Nana has everything she needs for the customers when they come and thru pick up. I make my way to the door to the back where she is. I know it's unlocked. Turning the hand and walking through closing it and walking passed the deep freezers and bread and pizza boxes. I was a few feet from Nana not to make her jump.

Emma: " Nana is just me". I say as I pull off my coat and lay it on the chair in front of the steel table.

Nana: "All right one mushroom sub anything else drive-thru pick up or kitchen. Alright, I will see you when you get here ." Nana hangs up the phone, pulls her washcloth from her shoulder and swings at me.

Emma: "Hey, I announced myself !"
Nana: " You scared me Emma dammit girl ".
Emma: "I am sorry Nana."
Nana: "What do you want, Emma?"

Walking over to the radio beside the phone I click it on and let the weatherman repeat what I just heard to my nana. Look at her and point to the sky or better the ceiling of the room.

Emma: "This is why I am here Nana, there is a blizzard. Why are you not home drinking coffee and getting ready to watch crime shows? I told you there was a documentary on Old Sparky ( the electric chair )."

Nana :" Emma, you don't tell me when to close up shop and go home. I am older than a dirt girl. I was driving in the snow before your mother even thought of it. Now sit down and let me make you some food

Ghosted Black Ice By D.Chaney

and you can try and boss me and try to get me to leave now when we both know I am the boss little lady. Know pizza or sub with fries, onion rings, breaded mushrooms, or okra."

Watching my nana with her short brown hair and her hands on her hips staring at me. Lifting her right arm, took her red nail-painted finger, and pointed it to the chair with my coat. Pulling it out and sitting down.

Emma: " You know me so well you pick." I say placing my hand on my stomach.

Nana: "Sub and mushroom and breaded okra then."

Nana knew what I liked and made her way back to the kitchen. I was not trying to control her. I wanted to keep her safe. She has had a hard life. Born in the hills of Kentucky in a cabin with no water or electricity. She was in a loveless marriage after she left my mom's father. Getting diagnosed with cancer, fighting cancer, and winning. All I do is worry for her nana was my babysitter when my mom worked. When I broke my arm Nana was there with me. My first dog Nana was there, her being here at the drive-thru in a blizzard. I would come and make sure she was safe.

I went to get up to go to the other side of the kitchen so I could talk to her. Before I could get up.

Ghosted Black Ice By D.Chaney

Nana: "Don't even think about lifting your ass off that chair Emma Park if you can nag after you eat."

Since I can't get up from the chair even though I am twenty-four. I turn to face her so I can try and make her see that I am not nagging but looking out for her.

I wait a few seconds watching Nana as she starts dropping food in the deep fryer and putting cheese on the subs and onions. Taking a deep breath I know this could be bad. I was the only brave one who would come and talk to her.

Emma:" I am not trying to nag you Nana I am trying to look out for you. I don't want you driving in the snow. Stay here there is food and drinks. The only thing you won't have is a bed. They say the blizzard can't give us a foot or more in snow. Please stay here if you can, especially if the snow is coming down hard ."

I know any minute now the clouds will let all hell loose on us. I know how far she has to drive. I have the same distance since Nana lives with us. I have 4 wheel drive on the Jeep that is why I bought it. If I asked her to come home with me now she would have my ass bent over her knee.

Nana: " I will think about it  Was it snowing when you pulled in?"

Ghosted Black Ice By D.Chaney

Emma:" No, but the radio said any minute now the snow will start and to get some. I already know you won't leave with me or let me follow you so I won't ask. I just ask if it's bad, please stay here."

Shutting the oven doors and walking to the dryer she looks over at me. "I said I will think about it. Know when my granddaughter is going to find a man."

Well, shit she's going for blood. " I don't need a man, Nana. I am good with my career now."

Nana:" Emma, when was the last time you got some good dick in your life? I know for a fact there has not been any man in your life. Get out there and spread your wings and your legs, you're being a mother these days. As your nana, I have to say practice safe sex young lady."

Yep, Nana was out for blood. It might have been since I was eighteen with my so-called ex-boyfriend but lesson learned. I won't do that again. I might need therapy for relationships cause I rather be alone than with someone. My ex didn't hurt me. I am the one who ended it. I guess seeing my nana's relationship and her and papal divorcing left a mark on me. I don't mind the pain, I don't want the effort and time that could be wasted.

Nana:" Emma, get out of that head of yours. Just cause you and your papal wasted so many years not loving one another doesn't mean you should stay single. For a fact, I feel that your life is about to change very soon and you will be having those cobwebs in your pussy cleared out from all the dick you will be getting ."

"Nana! Good God would you stop." All her straightforward and blunt talk can make you embarrassed and completely utterly shocked. What do I say after that speech about my crotch, dicks, and cobwebs?

She is just standing there putting my food in the paper containers now. With a smirk on her face, I had to ask her a thought.

"Was it work all those years being there in a loveless marriage." She places my food in front of me and walks to the door to head to the drive-thru where the coolers of pops and other drinks are. She doesn't stop to answer me. A few seconds later she is back with a drink placing it beside me.

" I would not have the life I have known and the knowledge I do. Who would have known how things would have turned out if I stayed married to your mother's father and not remarried into a loveless marriage? If you were here I would be stable in finances. We can't stay in the what if we keep in the know and make strides. Now eat your food. Oh whatever you do, don't run away, stay and be brave my girl. You never know when you will find the one

Ghosted Black Ice By D.Chaney

you're meant to be with." She walks back to the kitchen and works some more.

I had to say it. "What if I don't want to love Nana? What if I want to live my life single and painlessly do what I want when I want with no one to tell ."

Nana:" Love and relationships are not like that just because I left one man and ended up in a loveless marriage doesn't mean you will ."

Deciding to keep my mouth shut on the whole thing. Looking down, I see Nana made my favorite besides the pizza. A mushroom sub with extra mushrooms. The smell was heaven of a man could make this meal. I might think about the whole relationship.

The first bite is what is most important, always on the corner or the goods will come out on the sides. Letting out a moan stomping my food and pure love for this sub.

"Now if only we could get you to moan like that for a man and his dick." She just had to say something nearly choking on my heaven-sent sub. Just rude, just rude.

She got jokes so do I "So when are you going to get back on the wagon Nana? It's time for you to get a man." Shot fired Nana miss talk about sex and dick.

" I'll have you  know that I am too old for that shit." Just cause she did it to me.

Ghosted Black Ice By D.Chaney

" You're never too old for some dick Nana ". With that, I ate my food before she whooped my butt.

Standing up from the chair I pick up my now empty food containers and toss them into the trash. I rarely do this because it's her place. Stepping into the kitchen I walk to Nana putting my hand on her back.

" Please be safe Nana and if it's bad stay here please." Hugging her to hold her before I take off cause I am lucky the storm has not hit yet. Looking

out the window by the oven I can still see the road.

" Fine, I will if it's bad now, I have work to do. Take

the box of gummies and a few drinks with you just in

case and I will see you tonight or tomorrow."

Looking at the counter where I pick up, I see a box

that pops in a bag along with another bag. I kiss her

on the cheek and a hug. Going back to the chair I

pull my coat and scarf from the chair. Pulling my

gloves from my pockets as I walk back to the pick-up

counter on the other side shutting the door to keep

people out. Standing there looking at Nana across

the counter. I know she will watch me leave. Picking

up the three bags now.

Ghosted Black Ice By D.Chaney

" Well, Nana I will see you, I love you ". She waves her hand in the air toward the door. She always hated goodbye. With bags in one hand and opening the door to the parking lot. Looking back at her "Bye Nana" looking out the door to my car the cold wind hit me right in the face unlocking my car to get in. I place the Goodies on the back floorboard of my jeep.

Chapter Two - Dead Battery

Emma

Sitting in the driver's seat of my car while it warms up. Leaning to look in the rearview mirror, my brown eyes and my hair looking back at me. I hate this face. I hate what it brought into my life. The beauty pageant I did as a child made this face known, and you are supposed to look a certain way. Retired when I was young so the world and society couldn't eat my soul. I thank the universe that my mom had the trophies, ribbons, etc removed from the cabinet at the drive-thru.

Ghosted Black Ice By D.Chaney

Reaching to grab a scrunchie from the gear shift to put my hair up. Putting my hair in a messy bun so that it will last till I hit the shower. Looking back to the door I just came out of. I ask the universe to keep Nana safe. Buckling my seat belt and looking out the rearview mirror and on the sides, I put the car in reverse.

Turning right on the main road to the state route is what hurts me the most. What used to be a donut shop is now a restaurant. The trailer park that I've been in a few times. Stopping at the main light, I see my mom's old high school driving pass. There are so many memories on this road, a lifetime's worth. The second trailer park is another place I have been to a few times. The bingo hall and across from that is my most painful memory, my papal's mobile home sales lot. Everything is gone now, just the old sign hangs on the light pole. Burn to the ground was one of the most expensive fires, millions, they said.

I remember sleeping in Papal's office after he and Nana divorced. Him cooking beef jerky and letting me roam on the roads. Watching old TV shows on a small TV in the bedroom. Two family pets are buried on the hill. Going next door and got ice cream and papal telling me it would be his last one since he was a diabetic. So many memories on one little road. Papal is in Florida now for the winter. He will be back when the weather is sunny, or he wants to build another house or project.

Ghosted Black Ice By D.Chaney

Taking the curve to get on the state route the snow starts to hit, big flakes start to drop from the clouds. White cotton candy looking down at the dash, it's twenty degrees. The snow is going to stick. A straight line from here and I will be home. Nana's words hit me. You find a man like where on the side of the road I work all the time at my photography business. The wind is picking up and the snow is coming down. I can't see in front of me. I can't see in front of me, I am in a white, putting my hazard lights on. Feeling like the snow and the jeep are closing in on me, I know I should not do this. I know this was a mistake. My heart is racing in my chest, and it's getting harder to breathe. Dots appear in my vision. I need to catch my breath, pulling to the side of the state route, and closing my eyes to count. Ten nine eight seven six five four three two one. I repeat till my heart is calm, and I feel safe to open my eyes. The little black dots from earlier are gone now.

Looking back to the road, I can't see anything in front of me, but I need to get back on my route. Seeing as there was no one that I could see. I go to pull out and a deer is looking in my mirror and I see a deer beside my jeep. Well, if something was going to give me a scare, I am glad it was a deer. I look at it to see if it's going to move, and it just stares at me when one TikTok song pops into my head. The deer and I are just looking at one another. The deer moves to my window like it wants to face off. Its ears are twitching.

Ghosted Black Ice By D.Chaney

Grabbing my on the hot camera, I slowly work it on, so I can't take a picture. Not a damn soul will believe me that I had a face-off with a deer. Working the settings to turn off the flash pulled the camera up to my face, so I could see the deer through the camera. It has not moved, still looking at me twitching its ears. I take as many shots as I can as the deer moves and I swear it poses for the camera pointing its face up to the sky and letting the big snowflake land on its nose. Another round of photos taken feels like he or she wanted to be found by a human. The deer perks up and moves to the hood of my jeep pulling the camera from my face to watch where he or she goes. The woods are focused on the woods. Looking at the body of the deer I see a black heart on the side. Pulling up the camera, I take a few shots of the deer of hearts.

Before I know it, the deer runs off into the whiteout, and I am more than sure it went back into the woods. Placing my travel camera back into the center console. Looking over to the woods that I could see since I was in the middle of a white-out, I wanted to make sure the deer was safe in the woods and not going to come running back. Look in the mirrors putting the jeep in the drive when the lights go out and so does my dash and my car completely shuts down. Putting the car in park I try to restart nothing, no light, no repose. Slamming my hands on the steering wheel in frustration, my dad just checked my damn battery this morning. It feels like there is a cloud of fucked up shit happening lately.

Reaching for my bag in the backseat, brings it up to the front seat to search for my cell phone to call a tow truck or my dad. Pulling my phone out of my purse, I hit the side button and nothing. Pushing in the side but nothing, the red battery flashing sign appeared: the phone is dead. Putting my phone back into my purse, it's not like I could charge the damn thing. Leaning my head down on the steering wheel, I had to think of something.

That's when it hit me, with the snow emergency tote in the trunk. The one mom made me come back for this occasion. It has everything in except the jumper

I took it out this morning when I cleaned the trunk. "You're an idiot, Emma idiot, you also are talking to yourself out loud." Bundling my hands and putting the hood up, I unbuckled my seat belt and counted to three. " One, two, three, opening the driver door in a hurry and shutting it to keep the warm in. I rush to the trunk and hit the bottom button. Snow is slamming on my face, and the wind chill is a bitch. The wind picks up in a gush, and it almost takes me to the ground, grabbing the side of the jeep to keep sturdy. I grab the bags with the other, waiting till the wind calms down when I shut the trunk and bolts to the driver's door.

Slamming the door shut after throwing the bags into the passenger seat. Taking my gloves off I start

Ghosted Black Ice By D.Chaney

blowing hot air on my fingers. Opening up one of the duffle bags I find a big plush blanket, a hand warmer, candles, extra socks, a flashlight, and a first aid kit. Grabbing the handle of my seat, I pushed it back. Taking my shoes off, I grab the dried socks and replace the wet ones. Taking the blanket from the duffel bag and draping it over my legs to keep warm. Opening the second duffle bag there is food and drinks Nana must have packed this there candy bars and a can open for corn. Yep, she packed this there a thing of pepper spray with a note around.

*In case you forget you have a vagina and need protection. Don't worry about condoms there here as well. Now get some dick, my girl.*

She didn't lie there was a box of condoms in the duffle along with tampons, underwear, and deodorant. Looking out the window, the snow has not let up, it looks like it has gotten worse. A snow plow should be making its rounds soon. Keep positive someone will find me soon and help me with a jump. Leaning back in my seat, all that I can do is wait for help and see if anyone shows up. Tonight was not my luck, but at least I got to see that strange deer with the heart on its side.

Covering my hands in the blanket and tucking my feet under my butt like a little ball, I didn't want to use the candles until it was the last resort.

Ghosted Black Ice By D.Chaney

Chapter Three- Missed Flight

Kris Storm

This fucking computer every time I type it's messing up the word. How the hell did I end up doing the reports? It's usually Jasper who does them since he is the tech guy in the group, but no. I lost a bet on how long it would be before I broke my cell phone. I can't help that I and electronics don't mix. I don't have the temper for this. Pushing the back button for the hundredth time to fix my report on our last client. A famous male model had a crazy female stalker. The three of us hate the job, but it has been what we're good at.

The others in our group, Miles, a warlock, is a
doctor. Miles loves to help others with both his
skills, his craft, and medical training. Leo, a vampire
like the bloodsucker, is a lawyer. Since his battle
days. are over, he battles the criminals and evil
through the court system. Since he can't drink from
humans since the blood bag act happens in the
supernatural world. Leo gets his kills and thrills
from the wins in court. Felix the Demon is a
world-renowned chef. He says he is a chef so he can
eat as much. The hungry bastard.

So we all decided to come to the cabin for the
holiday. We all had a hand in making this cabin,
from the wood chosen to the plants outside in the

garden. There was only one level in the house empty and when that person arrives we all will move here. It might look strange and off. Humans have always looked at supernatural bones mates as something else. We are all bonded as brothers. Hell, we grew up together when we all turned eighteen we all decided to become bonded. We've been friends since we were in diapers. So when Jasper, Frost, and I needed a pack, we added our friends' soul contract as brothers. Three werewolves who run security and protection. A warlock, vampire, and demon. There is only one current problem: two of those idiots missed their flight and the others were delayed. Waiting for word if they got a flight, Jasper, a nervous cook, made cookies and now what smells like beef stew. I offered the asshole a switch but no he told me he won the bet, so I am fucked.

Slapping my hand down on the counter, I have to retype the same word six times. How in the hell did I type the word in all caps, unspaced, add letters, a number like what the fuck, then misspelled the word. I am half tempted to throw this laptop out the window and into the snow. I just fucking hate computers, this is more again Jasper's thing, he is the best.

I was about to ask Jasper to fucking do all this paperwork since he could have it done in less than ten minutes. The screen goes black on the laptop here the fuck we go again what button have I clicked, now. I flipped the laptop over to show Jasper

Kris:"Jasper, look at what the fuck this stupid thing is doing now."

He looks over at the laptop like the son of a bitch that he is and starts laughing at me. Jasper points to the screen .

Jasper: "The guys are calling, hit the green button, Kris".

I do as he says, I hit the green buttons and the screen starts filling up with boxes of our other bond mates. Seeing the three of them are still at the airport. I can hear the sound of the airport speakers through the laptop speakers. Five days till Christmas and these three are stuck all over the place. The guys have to make it, we don't celebrate Christmas without one another. Frost had stopped punching the bag and was not making his way over to the computer. Looking up, Jasper just keeps chopping, not bothering to slow down. There is no point in wasting time and not asking what we all need to know.

Kris:"Tell me you three have a way home,"

I said this is the stupidest thing they have done. I warned them last week they should have stayed home. Nope, not these idiots they knew better than anyone that never leave the week before Christmas week but nope the damn fools can't listen. Now they are stuck and wishing they were here. The folks decided to go down to Cocoa Beach for the winter, since they all have been close since before we all were born.

Ghosted Black Ice By D.Chaney

I figured I would start with the one that annoys me the most, well they all annoy me with this little stunt. Looking at the shaggy blond-haired man with blue eyes looking like he just got done surfing. That warlock bastard Miles and thin and muscular he has always been that way he has not worked out a day in his life, lucky son of a bitch. Miles last week decided to attend a last minute doctors conference in California. If he was the guest speaker, ok, but this was just info bullshit. I swear, this man would do a hand sanitizer conference if he thought it would better the hospital. Looking at the screen at Miles, he knows I want him to tell me what the fuck has happened. I know he didn't miss his flight because he was playing in some pussy at the hotel or the hospital. I bet he forgot to set the alarm on his phone for the flight.

Miles:"Well, I'm on standby for the next available flight to Ohio," Miles spoke up.
Shaking my head I look over to Leo who in their right mind would also mind you pulling a stunt like this. Leo decided to take a call from his client who lives in Florida. I hope he gets a sun Leo burns on his pale ass. Watching through the screen as Leo fixes his well-tailored suit.

Leo: "Unfortunately, gentleman, my flight is delayed, and I also am on standby. This is the most disorganized airport I have been to."

Ghosted Black Ice By D.Chaney

Looking closely at Leo with his black hair slicked back I can tell and so can the others he needs to feed, his hair is dull gray looking. There are deep purple half-moons under his eyes. His eyes have a red tinge in the white he is starving.

Frost lets out a sigh.

Frost: "Leo, when was the last time you fed."

Leo shifts in his seat. He Hungary alright and unfortunately.

Leo: " I have not eaten since I left the house ."

That was last Monday, which was six days ago. He knows better what is wrong with these guys.

Frost the less dick head of the group speaks again,

Frost:"Leo you need to eat buddy you are not looking so good and I can tell from here that you are weak."

Leo:"Well, you know the blood delivery service will not bring bags of blood into highly populated areas. I am on standby and I don't want to miss the chance to get the next flight out. I am fine, I can wait till I get home."

Kris: " You are being stupid."

Letting the other handle this so I don't lose my cool. Jasper:"The airport should call you when the next possible flight out so why don't you book a hotel room and go eat if then you feel the need to come back to the airport? we don't need you sticking your teeth into someone " Jasper stated while slowly cutting the food we all know why he wants to be silent.

Ghosted Black Ice By D.Chaney

Miles:"Yeah, man go ahead and get a room so you can hear there is no reason why you shouldn't. Don't worry we all will make it home for Christmas." Miles says.

Felix:"Dude don't be stupid you need to eat, listen you stubborn vampire ass hole," Felix irritation clearly can be heard in his tone.

We all watch as Leo pulls his phone from his pocket. He moves his fingers over the front of the phone. He keeps his phone in his hand when the phone lights up. Leo holds up a finger and puts us on mute, his screen goes black.

Felix: "Before we hyper-focus on Leo's not eating I am all so on standby I am about to head to the hotel in the airport, so I am not far. The food is dreadful, by the way. Jasper, are you using my knives? I know you think you are being coy by doing it slowly, but I can hear it, you shithead. I bought cheap knives so you and the others can use those, not my high-end knives."

Felix was close to the camera, I could swear he was about to crawl out of that little box. Looking over at Jasper I can see he has one of the knives in the air making hand gestures.

Jasper: "How can you tell that I am not using the cheap ones Felix you can even see me or the knives."

Ghosted Black Ice By D.Chaney

Felix:" Jasper, take those knives and put them back where you got them now. Use the family ones that you bought. Come on Jasper don't annoy me while I am states away. Felix the red-haired green eyes six foot four, built like a truck. Felix looks like a bodybuilder. His red face was as mad as the demon he is, more the chief in his was mad that his knives were being used. Felix was stuck in Arizona, where he offered to supply the catering to one of his cousin's weddings.

Felix:" Now Japer was and put my knives up."

After years of knowing these guys I can tell their next move Jasper was going to be an ass. lifting my head from the laptop I see Jasper walk over to the sink and turn in the water while washing the knife nope he is pretending to wash it. Looking back down at the screen I can see that Felix is running his

hands through his red hair, his signs of annoyance

heard through the screen. Felix's nose is flared and

his green eyes turn red.

Felix: "Japer I will suck the soul out of your body if

you don't listen to me." Felix's voice was more

demonic than his subtle tone.

Looking over at Miles I can tell he knows that Jasper

did this to get under Felix's skin. I can see on the

screen that Frost is shaking his head and this time

when the sink turns on I know that Jasper is washing

it this time. Felix lets out a sigh of relief. Leo pops

back onto the screen from what it looks like he is walking through the airport.

Leo:" You guys are right, I need to feed so I booked a hotel room and talked to the nice lady at the service desk and she texted me when I could get out of there. I am going to keep you all on the phone in case I am about to lose control."

It looks like Leo has put us in his pocket. Leo is not a place I want to be but hey. Looking over to Felix the color on his face is back to normal and so is his eye, if he were to lose control his horns would have come out. He's looking down at something, must be a recipe or something else, who knows what. Looking away to look at Miles he is in a frozen state not blinking or moving he must be having a vision or his guides are telling him something, he freaks me out when he does this. This is a blessing and a curse like the time when Jasper was almost shot by a client, Miles called to tell us that morning, and we were able to stop. The curse part is he is not able to tell when they will come.

Like a pop, Miles is out of the trance that he was in.

"Something is coming brothers, I don't know what it is but something big". We all take note of what Miles said. Jasper puts Felix's knife back into the cabinet, walks over to the family ones and continues to make the beef stew.

Chapter Four - Mate In the Air

Kris

The wind outside picked up the white snow covered trees beside the house, tree branches were scraping against the side of the house and windows. I could hear the gush of winds as they whipped through the trees and ran alongside the house . Jasper has been cooking for hours and got the stew on the stove. There was something about the moment, my heart picked up with the next gush of wind that smacked along the house and threw the small openings that let air in the house , and then it hit me. The scent of my mate hit me full force. Sugared strawberry with a hint of milk chocolate covering.

The shift happened so quickly, that my canines popped out of my gums. My vision got this red haze, I needed to find them, my mate. With a somewhat none-beast mindset, I stood from the chair and started moving to the door. It was not until my hand was on the knob that I realized that Frost and Jasper were behind me. More like running into one another with my face smashed into the outside I could see the snow coming down hard when I remembered there was a blizzard outside. I was sucked into the mate bond that I was about to go out in the snowstorm with nothing on but my shorts.

Pushing myself off the door I turned to the others,

we all knew that scent was our mate.

Looking at each other, we all three said:


MATE !!

Shaking my head to get some release from the still

lingering mate scent. The need to mate and mark

her surge through my core.


Kris:" We need to put some clothing on, the weather

is shit outside."


I don't know how I managed to walk away from the

door, or how I can get dressed. But I did my wolf

wanted to shift fully and scent the tail to my mate

Ghosted Black Ice By D.Chaney

Miles

It was like they guys had been hit in the face with the most Divine scent on the earth, I watched Kris and Frost change in their demeanor, and the bodies started shifting.

I watch as their canines come out in length,their usual color of golden honey hue eyes has changed to something more. Their eyes changed from golden wolf eyes to a snow white with a magical glow to them. I don't even think they realized that their nails have grown to their more beast nature. The way they are changing would almost make us think they would be in danger. I have never seen a guy's act like this. They have the same look of need and want. We all have seen them in their full moon state. But it was not the moon that was weeks ago, so I can't contemplate what is going on with the guys at home. Shifting in my seat and doing a quick look around the airport to make sure there is no one looking and being nosey. The only other possible thing it could be is our mate. Years of knowledge and education says a mate changes the dynamics of their said mates. The mate that is sent for all of us we all enjoy each other's scents, so we are boned pack mates. Three werewolves, a vampire, a warlock, and a demon. The sound of what would be three wolves abandoning everything and rushing to what I think is the door they guys sound, sounds more like a horse. There is a thump and everything stops. All I could hear from their end was the sound of deep breaths. I can't say how long it was, but I waited and watched a now blank screen . The hair on my arms and the back of my neck stand up. I heard it loud and clear, the one word that can make my skin glow green and have my whole body vibrate.

The one word that starts the bond even miles away.

"Mate !"

In the last bit of awareness, I hear Kris yelling for the others to get dressed.

I don't know how I ended up on the private bench in the airport bathroom. Looking down at my hand, I see a red rose of love and passion, my other hand still holds my phone. With the rose in one hand, I look back at my cell phone, I don't know how long I have been in the haze. I see Frost jumping around trying to put his pants and sweatshirt on at the same time, damn fool. I already know that it will not do any good to call out or ask questions, the guys won't hear me. They are in the mate haze. All focus is on finding our mate and bringing her home. Once they lock on her scent, they will do everything to find her for us all.

I need to be there with the guys looking over to Felix who now looks to be sitting on a bed. His eyes are blood-red you can only see the black pupils, the side of his head his horns are out and flared back. It's the look on his face that has me worried. The look on his face is sinister. He knows I do what our bond brothers have found. I need to calm him down before he goes into a demonic rage.

Miles:" Deep Breath my brother, deep breathe Felix, come on, breathe with me. We will be with our mate soon, but just stay calm."

Taking a deep breath and keeping my eyes on him. Leo still has not come back on the screen. I hope he orders a cooler fool so he doesn't end up at the brink like Felix, instead he will be bloodthirsty. The three of us need to get home as soon as possible, tucking the rose in my pocket, so I can give it to my mate when I see her. I stand from the bench and make my way back to my seat. I am not calm, but I am stable to be around people.

Frost

Hat, Jacket socks, and shoes. I am all good-looking around, where the hell are the other two idiots? I don't have to guess, looking at the sound of crashing through the cabin and then cursing. Jasper comes storming down the stairs and flies into the kitchen like his ass is on fire. Another crash comes from someplace further into the cabin, and then what sounds like a stamp. The smell of our mate was starting to fade away. These fucking idiots need to speak the fuck-up and let go. Jasper walks over to the stove and turns it off. Thanks to the moon, I forgot about the stove being on. I don't have time to waste. I make my way to the front door this time with no roadblock. I am not wasting time the others

Ghosted Black Ice By D.Chaney

are behind me or not and can catch up with me. Opening the front door I step out into the snow and the cold out mate scent is still strong out here. Lifting my face I take a big breath into focus on her scent like before sugared strawberries with a hint of chocolate. I hear the others take in a deep breath along with me doing the same things as getting the mate's scent locked in. My wolf is trying to come out. "Mate is coming from the woods on the right." he lets out a growl in my head, he is ready to make our mate ours to feast on their body. I moved to the woods and my brothers followed. The wind is hitting my face like a demon trying to get inside and corrupt my soul. I know I have seen Felix do it a few times in the past. The lights from the cabin began to fade as we made our way further into the woods. Every few feet, we stop and take in a deep breath to get a better idea of where our mate is. The snow has caused and glows around the trees. We keep focused on the scent and keep walking into the woods silent, nothing what it should be since the snow storm has caused the road route to be dead silent just the wind and our breath is the sound. The scent of our mate gets even stronger with each step I take, and I know my brothers can smell it as well. I keep looking and walking through the break in the trees. Stepping out from the trees, I see a jeep parked on the side of the road. It's the only vehicle I can see. The jeep is covered with snow. Most of the jeep is almost hidden in the snow, all but the windshield.

Jasper

Ghosted Black Ice By D.Chaney

My brothers and I break through the trees. All I can see with the wind and snow hitting my face is a Jeep. Statistics say that jeeps are good for driving in the snow. I can see the windshield cleared off. I could not stop myself. I made my way through the snow to the front of the jeep. Mate scent is the strongest here, looking through the window I see a woman through the darkness of the vehicle. Stopping to stare at the beauty that is our mate. I could spend days just looking at this beauty. We all have waited for her since we all turned the age of eighteen. Going straight for her door but finding it locked.

"Locked"

The others don't even ask if they know I can open the door.

Opening one of the many programs I have designed, making quick work, I can the VIN and override her system to unlock the doors. It takes seconds to do. The sound of the doors unlocking fills me with some much pleasure. I am the one who can save her from the snow without damaging her property. Dusting off the snow on the driver's side window from chin down, she is tucked in a blanket. Not wanting to scare her if I open the door. I tap on her window and our mate moves, but only to bury herself more into the blanket. Giving her a few seconds and tapping again and not getting any movement from her.

Taking a deep breath I opened the door wide Frost was behind me Kris was beside me doing his best with his body to block out the wind from touching

Ghosted Black Ice By D.Chaney

our mate. Her scent hit me hard and made me hard. Pure luck and miracle did are mate get stopped on the side of the road and have the wind bring us together. My brother and I smell the hint of her fertile pheromones in the car, and my brother moves us closer to her side.

Reaching out to check her neck for a plush. Her heart rate is steady and strong. Looking down at the key ingestion, I see the keys, plus I don't have to be inappropriate to search her.

I pulled her from the driver's seat, keeping the blanket wrapped around her. Kris opens the door behind me and quickly steps back to give me and our mate room. Placing her in the back seat. Shutting the door and making my way to the passenger side of the car. Climbing into the back set with closing the door. Frost is already in the driver's seat. He turns

the key to the car and it starts up automatically

checking the four-wheel drive is on. Frost is messing

with the dials on the console. Kris is scrapping the

windows so we have a clear view before long he gets

the passenger seat and shuts the door. I grab our

mate and put her head in my lap. We have a hidden

drive well know that's hidden just have to know what

to look for to enter.  Running my fingers through her

hair, her scent comforts me and puts me at ease.

After the car is warmed up,  Frost puts the car in

gear and we slowly and steadily start to drive back to

our cabin. I look out the window and I see the

strangest thing, a deer looking our way with a heart

near It's but.


Ghosted Black Ice By D.Chaney

Pulling up to the cabin I have never been happier that we started building this when we were eighteen. Everything my mate will need and or kids. Secluded from the rest of the world surrounded by mother nature, big open windows show lights from when we left. Six bedrooms for each of us, one kitchen, and one living room with multiple coaches. One master bedroom with a custom-made bed for when she came. The room has been locked up for many years, but now we will all be moving into that room. There are so many rooms it is not a cabin but a mansion, but we all call it the cabin since the outside is made of logs. The back of the house has a poolroom with an open concept where you could swim and watch the snowfall or take a dip in the hot tube. I hope she likes her new home pulling her close, Frost turns off the Jeep. Frost is out and has our mate's door open. " you guys get her stuff while I get her comfortable in the living room."

Frost shuts the door and takes off to the door to the cabin where I can see him open and close with her in arms bundled up.

Looking around the jeep I see a bag on the back driver floor floorboard. I see a bag of sorts with the smells coming from the bag, it will be her food. Not seeing anything else, I open the door and step out. Kris has his arms full of her things not bothering to look at the back of the jeep. I push the lock button on the door and start to make my way to the cabin.

Ghosted Black Ice By D.Chaney

## Chapter Five - Dreams of Touch

The subtle touch

Warmth spreading to my toes

engulfing me in warmth

Chipping at my walls

Inch by inch

The grumble at my feet

Linking my soul to theirs

No matter how hard I try, my walls are gone

Devotion, love, peace, protection

Six souls are now mine until my end

I am there's

Bites, Blood, Tattoo, and burning

marks

Mark to show who I belong to

Chapter Six - Leo's mate on the other side

Leo

I arrive at the hotel and check into my room. As soon as I get into my room I have my blood app open placing a cooler order. The blood will arrive in about fifteen minutes. I am hungrier than I thought. I can't talk or be bothered to go back to my video chat with my brothers. Placing my phone on the table in the hotel room I sit down on the couch closing my eyes and taking deep breaths, my teeth pop out of my gums. Cutting my bottom lip with their points, the scent of blood makes me hungrier by the second.

A surge of need and want and blood hits me all at want my cock goes hard, and I want to feed and fuck.

Ghosted Black Ice By D.Chaney

I want my mate. I want to drink from her clit while she cums all over my face. Primal need rushes through me images of her coated in blood riding my cock as her blood drips onto our joined bodies, The more I think the more I get hard and thirsty. My mate sucking my sick while my other brothers fuck her pussy and ass while I shoot my cum down her throat I need to stop these thoughts. Standing from the couch I start packing and counting TV couch repeats.

I reach one thousand passes when there is a knock on my hotel room. Walking to the hotel room I look through the peephole to see who it is. It's the blood delivery service opening the door. I hold my breath so the hint of blood doesn't hit me in the face and have my teeth at this woman's neck. She handed me the cooler and I went to turn away from her when she reached her hand out, reaching toward me and running it down my chest.

Delivery Lady:" You're my last delivery for the day. If you're looking for some fun I am free."

I can feel myself starting to get in a bloodthirsty rage. How dare this woman think it's okay for her to put her hands on me when my body and mind think that we have found our mate and it sure the fuck is not this tuna casserole-smelling woman bitch mate. I rip her in half and bathe in her blood. This filthy fucking bitch she don't know I would shredd her up like a cat to a post.

Ghosted Black Ice By D.Chaney

Leo :" No thanks." My teeth feel like they're going to crack with all the pressure I have on them. I am trying not to pull her into this hotel room, sink my teeth in the artery in her neck.

Delivery Lady:"Don't be shy I bet we could have a lot of. How about you invite me in and let me take care of you." This woman proceeds to touch the waist pants of my pantsuit. Reaching down I snatch her hand up in a hard tight grip that I know will be leaving a bruise. I hear the sound of breaking bones and know I broke her wrist. She lets out a wine and tries to snag her wrist out of my hand but I hold it longer. Just because she is a woman does not give her the right to ignore the word no. Letting her wrist go I grab her face so she looks at me. She has tears running down her face black makeup streaks running along her cheeks.

Leo: " I will not say this again but the answer will be no, I would advise you to get a better profession if this is how you are going to act to customers. You might as well be on the corner with all the cheap pussy.  I will make sure to inform your place of employment of your misconduct."

Pushing her shoulder so she knows out of my doorway and further into the hallway. With one final look at the woman, I slammed the door shut and slammed the security lock in place.  Turning left to

Ghosted Black Ice By D.Chaney

go into the bathroom I place the cooler on the bathroom sink. As quickly as I can I strip out of my clothing. Placing them on the tool furthest from the shower. Opening the cooler pulled out the bagged blood and put it in my mouth to sink my teeth in. I grab the cooler and make my way to the shower as I put it on the shower seat, I turn the water on hot. Turning so the water will mainly focus on my back drinking the blood bag slowly. I pull the cooler open again to get a new bag of blood when the hint of sugary strawberries with chocolate hits my nose. My cock is hard and before I could stop myself I ripped open a bag of blood, having it pour all over my cock throwing the empty bag to the floor of the shower . Wrapping my hand around my cock moving up and down letting  the blood coating my finger with the blood I move my hand up and down my cock I can't wait till it's my mate's blood that I get myself off to. I work by myself thinking of the things I want to do for my mate. The way I would give her pleasure. The mere thought of having her for a week to do and pleasure as I see fit has me cumming in my hand the smell of cum and blood keeps me cumming over and over. A red haze clouds my vision. I see deeper and deeper into lust and the need of blood.The haze sets in and before long I lose myself to the pleasure and feeding.

When I come out of the blood lust I am still in the shower with bags of blood around me. My hunger is stated well by one of them. At least the need to find my mate and have is still burning deep in my bones. Picking up the blood bag I place them back into the cooler. I clean the walls and the floors to make sure there is no trace of blood on anything. Taking a show myself I wash off the blood and the dirt using the horrible hotel soap.

Grabbing the towel that is hanging up to dry off. I dress quickly in a T-shirt and sweats. I have a deep feeling I am missing something that I should be a part of. Placing the cooler at the side of the hotel door so I can schedule them to come and pick it up. I walk over to the table where I left my phone and click on the video and the volume I see my other brothers looking as bad as me or

worse I see Felix's horns have come out.

I see Frost carrying in a woman he goes off-screen, so my thought is he is taking her to the couch. Just the sight of her long black hair has my body wanting to go into a bloodlust again, taking deep breaths I calm myself.

" What happened?" I ask.

Miles takes a sigh "She has come, brother."

Felix.: "While you were gone we were talking when Miles went blank and proceeded to say that something was coming good or bad he couldn't tell what it was either. Then the three mutts went all dog and said mate. You should have heard them; they

Ghosted Black Ice By D.Chaney

sounded like a bunch of horses. Then we had to watch one get dressed which was funny as fuck have you ever seen one of the guys try and put more than one piece of clothing on at the same time. Then they ditched us and they came back the same time you did."

Leo : "Wow !"

Leo: "Thanks for getting me up to speed Felix".

Miles: "Yep, that sums it up."

'The bad thing is we are all state away and missing out on the moment with her we have to get back home.' Felix, with a hint of anger in his tone.

Leo: "Frost shows us our mate."

Frost brings our little mate as close as he can to the laptop. She is all wrapped up. I can see her black hair cascading over Frost's arm. I could imagine having her long hair wrapped around the palm of my hand as I fuck her little pussy from behind. While her neck drips blood down her breast.

Frost doesn't stay in front of the camera there long. He moves off the screen back to place her on the couch. The sound of a door opening and you can hear the faint sound of feet coming into the room. I watch as the guys walk across the camera with bags of things. Kris noticed that we couldn't see our mate, and turned the camera toward the living room where we could see the fireplace and the couch.

Frost is tucking our mate into the couch covering her with the throw blanket, Kris and Frost take either side of her. I watch as she tries to snuggle into Kris's body to steal his warmth. Jasper is not on the screen but I can hear him closer than the rest, the opening of bags and the fridge.

Jasper: " Do you think the beef stew will be enough for when she wakes up, or should I make more food."

"Felix, what would you cook in this situation"

" Well this is not fancy but I would make her a peanut butter sandwich, no jelly" he grins like he is locked in a moment.

" Make her a hot chocolate," I say. A woman loves chocolate, and if it is cold outside it's a win-win.

"Put another blanket on her if her clothing is wet, you three need to change her out of them and into clothing. We don't want her to get sick" miles full on doctor mode.

Kris breaks from looking at our mate "We found her in the driver's side she is not wet. I mean she could be but not in a place where it is open".

Ghosted Black Ice By D.Chaney

Jasper: "Her shoes are wet, I felt them when I was putting her into the car."

Frost stands from the couch and walks to our mate's feet, untucking the blankets. I don't have a foot fetish, I say. Kris moves from her other side and just walks out of the room on a mission. I watch as Frost stares at her now bare feet.

Frost

Her little bare feet are in my hands is what is on them that has me in shock, I trace the ink. Little stars and the moon are on both of her feet. Six moons, three on each foot, I take my finger and trace one of the moons surrounding the moon. Her toes are painted in a deep blue, I wanted to suck these toes rubbing the base of her foot out little mate moves ticklish. I place her feet back on the lounge. I have never been happier that we custom ordered this couch with one lounge in the middle of three seats on each side, she is the center of our heart.

Taking my previous seat by her, taking in her scent, is what we all have been waiting for her. Kris comes into the room carrying a pair of socks. I watch, and I am sure the other ones on the laptop can see. Kris drops to his knees at the end of the lounge to put socks on our mate, the meanest son of a bitch, and I like his mother.

Ghosted Black Ice By D.Chaney

I once watched this ass whole beat the shit out of a man because he took the last ice cream he wanted. Here he is on his knees before our mate being as gentle as he can't be putting her socks on her feet.

" We need to get home as soon as we can" I hear Felix say, there is a hint of jealousy in his voice.

Kris turns his face to the laptop, "Soon brother, you will be here to join us".

Looking beyond the laptop, I can see Jasper opening a bag that was still on the counter, it's from our mate's car. He pulls out the aluminum foiled object. I watched as he unwrapped them and saw him smile and smirk. " Oh Felix, you are going to have a challenge on your hands, our little mate-like mushroom subs." He let out a little snicker as he wrapped it back up and went to the fridge.

"From a place called Nanna's Drive Thru "Shaking my head, I already know when things settle down Jasper will have researched and looked into everything our mate likes to candy. I know like the others we can't wait to learn more about our mate and her likes and dislikes.

"Hmm, I will have to look into different recipes for her to try," Felix said.

"Check and see if she has a fever since she was out in the cold," Miles, the doctor, said.

Ghosted Black Ice By D.Chaney

I reach over and place my hand on her forehead, "She is fine" I tell them.

Kris reaches over and smacks me on the arm, "You're much hotter than her, she is a human, you idiot." Kris gets up from the couch and gives me his finger while he makes his way down the hall toward the bathroom.

Okay, maybe I was not thinking right, there has been a lot that has happened in a short amount of time.

Kris comes back with the thermometer on her head when the peep rings out "98.8 she is good".

" Good, just keep an eye on her temp and make sure it doesn't go too high since she was out in the cold, she can still get sick," Miles said.

" You were right Kris, it was a bad time to leave," Kris said, and the others shook their heads as well. I look down at my mate and I never would have thought waking up this morning I would be getting my mate, I can't help but be thankful for it as well.

Ghosted Black Ice By D.Chaney

Chapter Seven - Three Muscle Strangers

Emma

Warmth surrounds me snuggling in closer taking in the heat sources. The smell of marshmallows tickles my nose, I want to stick out my tongue and lick whatever it is that has this warmth. Realize that I am not in my jeep. Opening my eyes, moving myself back to the open space. Looking around, I see three males surrounding me. One on either side of me and another further down. All three of them are bulky, faint snores come from the three. I am most definitely not in my jeep standing up in a rush trying to get away from these three. My legs are tied up in the blankets, and before I can't stand, I am laid out on the floor. The sound of me falling must have woke them up.

Before I can even try to work my legs from the blanket, three heads come into view.

"Are you okay?" one asked.

"Did you hurt yourself?" another one asked.

The one that has not spoken has a resting asshole face. He just looks at me and starts pulling the blanket that is tangled around my legs.

I was just too stunned to speak. Looking around at the three and watching the one with the grumpy face. Finding my voice, "Hello" I never knew I had a weak voice until now.

The three start in rapid fire, and start talking.

"Hello my name is Frost, are you okay" the muscled blue-eyed short blonde hair asked.

"My name is Jasper do you need help" deep winter green eyes ask me looking at him, he has deep black hair.

The one with the grumpy face," I am Kris and don't be scared, we will not hurt you".

"How did I get here?" I asked them, I thought for sure I would have been woken up by a blow truck person or a cop doing some sort of public service.

Not three men on the couch.

Taking a deep breath, I don't even know if I want to ask but.

Emma:" How did I get here?"

The three of them look at one another like they're having a private conversation.

Kris, I believe, I am just going to call him Mr. Grump. I guess he was the one that decided to tell me.

"We found you on the side of the road". He cast a look of concern and I watched as his eyes traveled over my body before one of the others spoke.

Jasper: "We didn't want you to freeze, so we thought it was best to bring you here to our cabin."

Frost: "Your jeep is out front, you can leave anytime you want."

Kris: "The only problem is that the snow storms have the state in a level three, only emergency crews are allowed on the roads."

"So let me get this right you all decided I don't know, let's not call the police and get this woman help. Instead, you all find a way to get my Jeep started and bring me to a cabin" looking past them through a window," in the fucking woods. Now, this is not creepy at all to be here with three men. Let alone be stuck in here for who knows how long."

All I could do was laugh at the situation that I am in. How the hell did I end up in this mess?

"Stuck in the woods with strangers." I am more than sure I look like a mental case. Still sitting on the floor I make a move to get up, and Mr. Grumpy leans down. "Here let me help you up "Putting his hands under my armpits he lifts me like I am a child, and my feet dangle for a few minutes. Looking down between us, I can see the blanket pile up, but what I noticed more is his huge cock at attention. Looking back up at his face, I can see a scar on his brow line. I can see the pain in his eyes, the fear, and the anger. Licking my lips, Kris takes a step back from the blankets and sets me down on the floor. I watch as the other two stand from the floor trying not to look but could not help myself, their cocks are hard. My pussy is a fucking trader, she wants these three men so bad.

She is dripping, more like drooling with need and want. My mouth is watering to have a taste of each one of them.

"What would you like to eat for breakfast?" Kris asked as he moved closer to me, the smell of apples.

Looking at the big grump," I am not hungry, but thanks"

Grump looked at me and crossed her arms over hit chest" yea no I don't think that will work you're going to eat. So bacon, sausage, eggs, biscuits, and gravy."

He didn't even get me a chance to say no again before he had me up in his arms again and carried me over to the kitchen. The others followed behind, and Mr. Grump placed me down on one of the stools at the island. Looking around the kitchen with a built-in fridge and freezer, the stove is massive for three people. It's kind of an overkill. Dark marble and wood with silver appliances. This looks like a man's kitchen for sure or a group of men, not an ounce of color.

Who am I to judge, I live with my parents and Nana just in the basement, so I have more room and can come and go as I please.

Jasper and Frost start pulling things from the fridge and the cabinets. I look for Grump, and he is in the living room folding the blanket I was tangled in, it's like he can sense me looking at him, and he turns his head to the side. I can see the smile on his face from here. When he is done, he makes his way back over to the island, taking the seat next to me.

" So it's just the three of you that live here," I ask, looking out the window above the sink.

Jasper giggles a little before he says, "There are three others that live here, they just happen to be out of the state at the moment."

" So there are six of you that live in this " huh, trying to keep my mouth shut, no wonder this is everything in a bigger proportion.

Looking over to Jasper and Frost, I see the two almost run into each other, coming close to breaking the eggs.

"I am not hungry, it has nothing to do with you, it is all me. I don't eat at people's houses for a few days. It's just one of my quirks." I can feel my hands start to sweat from my nerves starting to get me worked up.

Jasper and Frost stop what they're doing and look at me. They both nod their head and smile at me. "Completely understandable, would you feel comfortable if you made the food you can show us how you like it." Jasper's tone is so soft as he asks me how I could tell him no.

"We can try "I get up from the stool and make my way around the counter. I take a deep breath. It is not that I am scared, it is the fact that I have quirks. Jasper and Frost part way so I can stand in between them. My stomach gives a rumble of hunger. I might as well ask them if they want me to cook them food as well since they let me cook food in their house.

"Do you three want me to make you some food as well?" I ask.

After the eggs are fried and the bacon is cooked,

each plate has some toasted bread. I place each of

the guy's plates in front of them.

Sitting back down at my place with my plate placed

before me. I don't even get to take a bite of food

before moans happen around the island.


I look at the guys, it's like they know when I am

looking, they start to talk. It would spook me if I

didn't feel comfortable with it.

" This is so much better than Felix's breakfast,"

Jasper says with a fork full heading to his mouth.

"The eggs are the right salt and crispy," Frost says

with his eyes closed.

"I can't wait to tell if he has been outcooled, "

Grump says with a smirk on his lips.


Ghosted Black Ice By D.Chaney

The smirk on my face must have gone unnoticed because I watched Grump eat and I mean he eats. I don't even think the man is breathing, I am shocked he is using eating utensils.

Eating slowly, I want to know about this Felix person," so is Felix your roommate."

"Yes, he is more like family, though," Jasper says.

"He is a chef, that's why we made all the food comments," Frost says as he gets up from his stool and makes his way over to the sink.

"Then there is Miles who is a doctor and Leo who is a lawyer."

Knowing that these three unknown males were not here with me makes my heart hurt.

Being polite, I give Jasper a warm smile," I hope they make it home before Christmas."

If they were not so stubborn and listened when I told them it was a bad idea to leave the state the week before Christmas, they would not be held up at the airport." I can tell Grump was pissed at them, his eyes turned to anger and his lips thin out, his ounce loose hand now fist around this fork and knife.

Looking back at my food, I continue to eat.

Finishing my last bite of food I go to clean my plate, but all three men are blocking me, Kris plucks my plate from my hand and Jasper takes my fork out of my hand and hands it to Kris.

Ghosted Black Ice By D.Chaney

" I am going to do the dishes, why don't you relax."

Frost and Jasper cough in their hands, eyes wide.

"Well, I am going to get some things done on the laptop. I will be there in a little."

Frost steps forward"Come, let's go, settle into the couch".

Frost put his hand on my back and guided me to the couch. He takes his hand from my back and snaps one of the throws from the back of the couch. The center of the couch has a little lounge seating. Frost pats the lounge. "This is where you sit."

I realize I have not told them my name in a gentle tone, "My name is Emma," I say, sitting down in my spot for the next few days. Frost covers me with the blanket and settles down beside me.

When I look over to the kitchen, Jasper's back is to me, I can see people on the screen and him whispering to them as he types on the computer.

"Want to watch TV ?'

"Yes, I would love to watch TV with you"

Frost leans over and picks up the remote.

"What do you want to watch," he asks, turning on the TV.

"Can we watch some ghost shows?"

"Of course, we can watch some."

Looking over at him, he is so handsome. I keep following his body. He shifts, and I look back up to his face. He was looking at me with a smile on his face. The ass has a cocky grin, lifting his brow.

"I like checking you out too, Emma."

He clicks some random show and puts the remote down. He leans down and near my head, I can feel his breath on my ear.

" You smell so good. I could lick you for days." I swear I could feel his tongue on my ear. The warmth of his tongue and he smells marshmallow, and it sends vibrations down to my toes. Causing my already unruly pussy to start drooling, she is hungry for some dick.

Taking a deep breath and trying to talk my pussy down. Traitor, she is dripping, I can feel my panties getting wetter by the second. Frost leans in and takes a deep breath. Before I could say anything, he pulled away and stood up.

"I will be right back, he said."

I watch as Frost stumbles from the couch and down the hall.

The sounds of coughing have me looking over to Jasper, a statue he doesn't look my way, "I am going to go check the mail." He walks over to the door and puts his shoes and coat on before opening the door and leaving. Looking back at the TV, why are they acting strange?

The sound of dishes dropping in the sink and the water splashing on the floor has me looking back over to the kitchen. Grump is standing there like a statue. He steps away from the sink and does the same thing that Jasper has just done. "Huh" Before

Mr. Grump shuts the door he says" I am going out to get wood, I will be back in a few."

Well, that was strange. Not bothering to follow any of them. They will sort it all out and come back to me. I do know I am going to have to take a shower, so I can get some release.

Chapter Eight - We are Cumming to the Woods

Frost

I could smell her, the sweet scent of strawberries and chocolate. The smell of her need to be aroused drove the wolf insane. We wanted to drink her release and have her pass out from pleasure. The pure agony it was to want to coat my dick in her juices. To watch her face as her walls tighten around me. I want to hear all her moans when I enter her and when our cums mix with one another.

I can imagine her on her knees with my cock in her mouth, perfect lips wrapped around my cock. The warmth of her mouth as she takes me into her mouth. I can feel her sucking in her cheeks and licking the base of my cock. The slurping and moans in the air, the pain as she digs her nails into my ass as she takes my cock further into her mouth.

So many things are running through my head, the sound of her choking, the feel of her swallowing all my cum. Knowing a part of me deep in her belly until she is pregnant.

I had to get out of the living room, her scent was making me mad, how could I have so many fantasies in a short amount of time? I could not face her any longer. Standing up from the couch, in a breathy voice, I tell her, "I will be right back." My feet barely keep me up trying to breathe, simultaneously wanting to inhale her scent. I could only imagine my appearance, focusing on my footing and not running into the walls. The nearest room was the bathroom.

Shutting the door, I lock it in case she comes looking for me. Finally, reaching out to the light switch, I flick the light on. Taking in a deep breath, I have never been happier to have that air freshener that usually messes with my senses.

The only way I could ease my torment from not being able to fuck my mate. Fucking myself and by the way, my body is acting like a teenager looking at a pair of tits for the first time. Walking over to the sink, I rather wash the cum off the sink, to have my cum all over the floor. Tuning on the water to muffle any sound that will come to the bathroom.

Pushing my sweat pants down I grab my cock and like before I let my mind wander to all the things I want to do to Emma. My beautiful mate laid out on my dark blue sheet. Looking at her face, her eyes have a hint of hunger and their teeth biting down on her lower lip. Moving down Emma's body her nipples are puckers peaks deep brown rounds licking my lips I want to suck on them little peaks to her moans. My eyes travel down her body, and their pussy comes to the site. Those pussy lips are wet and so is the spot on the bed.

I could see my other bond mates around the bed, Kris leans over the bed and sucks on one of her nipples. Felix comes to join on the other side, doing the same with her other nipple. Emma's eyes are closed as Felix and Kris suck on her nipples, watching as the little wet spot gets bigger. Leo comes to her side now and starts to spread her pussy lips, running his finger in a v. Her back lifts off the back, and she gives a moan in pleasure.

Jasper and Miles love to watch, so I know they are
already hand fucking their palms to our girl. With no
hesitation, I dive onto the bed, where Emma's pussy
was inches from my face. Looking up at Leo with a
wink, he knows what we are about to do. Leo spread
her pussy lips to where her clit was open and wanted
me to suck on and lick. I watch for a few seconds as
he rubs her pussy lips. Leaning forward, give her clit
a suck and put my index finger and middle finger
inside her. Nice and wet dripping with need, pulling
my fingers from her pussy I pull my lips from her clit
and stick my fingers in my mouth to suck the
strawberries and chocolate off. With a pop, I pull
them from my mouth and push my fingers back into
her. Working my finger in and out, sucking and
licking. I could not help myself grinding into the

Ghosted Black Ice By D.Chaney

bed, rubbing my cock on the sheets below me. I can feel the pre-cum leaking.

Her pussy tightened on my fingers. She is close to Cumming, and her walls are like suction cups trying to take my fingers further into her pussy.

I can feel myself about to come as well, the others might as well be in the same boat as me. Their moans and her last scream of realization does me in, long hot warm cum shoots out and puddles in the sink. In my head, my wolf howled he let me have this round but the next time he would take over to have what he has longed for.

Kris

Stepping out of the cabin, I could not take Emma's scent any longer.

Kris:"Deep breathe, Deep Breathe."

I am fighting with myself and my wolf to not go back into the cabin. I would spread Emma's legs and drink her nectar, I wonder if she is a squirter. Walking away from the front door the snow is up to my knees, the storm has done a number, what better than a shower of snow in negative temperature? Making my way through the cars, trekking through the snow to get to the woods. The further I walk into the woods, the further I get away from my mate's arousal. When I got a spot in the woods that I felt good in. I could not take it any longer, my wolf needs a loss. I don't care who sees me, I push down my pants and fist my cock. My breath puffed out as a little smoke, just showing how cold it was. I wonder if I will frostbite on my cock in the cold, I don't care, it is not going to stop me from this moment, or I will go in that cabin and have my mate. Closing my eyes like always, I let my thoughts run rapidly.

My little mate is running in the woods on the night when the moon is full and calling to us. The glow of the moon cast and glow gives off a spooky vibe. She was running from me, she knew that this would drive me mad. I don't know if she trips in the woods, or if she fakes it. She manages to get scratches, the hint of her blood in the air drives me mad.

Emma:"Oh fuck me."

Her voice pierces my pine as the sound of her defeat, she doesn't even attempt to get up from her hands and knees. I watch for a few seconds as her back leans toward the ground, and her hair is draped over her head.

The wolf in me takes over, "I plan to mate" ripping her leggings apart, I push her to the ground where her head lays flat on the. Her perky round ass in the air, her arousal, hits me hard in the face. The crotch of her pants ripped open her pussy shining in the moon, her wet little pussy dripping with need taunts me, the pussy lips calling for my tongue to lick them clean and nibble to have her shaking.I could not help myself. I smash my face into her pussy. I take in her strawberry and chocolate scent and she tastes just like she smells her juice just keeps dripping.

I could feel my k9 teeth grow longer, hanging above my lip. My wolf tongue comes out hanging, I part her pussy lips before my tongue goes into her perfect pussy hole. I wiggled my long tongue, licking her walls, sucking around her pussy hole to get her all of her taste. She pants and moaned as I worked my tongue faster and faster. Moving my tongue in a wave as I continue to suck and swallow all the juices from her pretty pussy taking in the sweet taste of her juice. I pull away from her before she can cum.

Kris: "You're going to fuck my face," I tell her. Turning around so I can lay on my back I drag her pussy across my face to smear her scent along with her fluids on my face. I pull her clit in my mouth so I can have a feast working the sensitive little flesh. Sucking her clit and pushing two fingers into her tight hole my wolf tongue didn't stretch her a bit. I can feel her getting more relaxed as she grinds her pussy across my face and lets more of her weight push down on my face. I pull my fingers out of her pussy and collect all the juices she has spilled. With my finger cover I move them to her tight little asshole  I push one finger into her . I can feel her tightening around my finger  still sucking her clit. I keep pushing my finger in and out of her asshole every time I pause with my finger out of her ass and push it back in she would moan. When she is loose around my finger I add a second finger she moans louder and pushes back onto my fingers. Pushing her away from my face "Come with my fingers in you tight little asshole" moving my fingers faster.

Her asshole tightened around my two fingers and she let out a long scream. Fluid comes rushing out of her pussy coating my face not able to handle it I push her back down on my face and start sucking and lick while I continue to fuck her little ass with my fingers. When she tightens around my fingers again I open my mouth and when that strawberry chocolate juice pours into my mouth I am in heaven. Her little body shakes so badly live this time she sounds like she is in front of me.

Emma: " Fuck me now "she says.

When the shaking has stopped I lift her up from my face and place my hand on her stomach with her pussy above my face, I move my other hand down to my jeans. I undo my pants and drag her down by spreading her pussy fluids along the way. body till her pussy juices were across my chest. Sitting here right above my cook, so I can sit up. Sitting up, I lift her back up above my cock.

Kris:"Do you want this cock baby?" I ask her, not letting her move. Looking up at her face, her pupils were blown with pleasure. Her dark black hair cascaded down her breast.

Emma:"Yes, give me it is hard" She leans down and kisses my mouth. She moans in my mouth and I know she can taste herself on me and it turns her feral as she tries to impale herself on my cock.

Still kissing her I looking over her shoulder, I can see the moon peeking through the trees. The moon has a second ring around it giving an even brighter glow.It's calling me pulling from her lips. She is perfect, she is mine and I will give her my all.

I slam her down on my cock down, till my cock can't go any further. Emma screams as she takes me in.

Ghosted Black Ice By D.Chaney

Her walls are tight around me, and she is shaking. I give her time to adjust to me. When her body has relaxed and her breathing has calmed down. I lift her until she is completely off my cock. I let her think whatever for a second before I slam her back down on my cock.

Emma:"Harder "she screams.

I slam into her until I can't any longer and the sound of slapping skin and her moans. I watch as her tits jiggle, her pace matches mine. I snagged one of her nipples and sucked as I continued to ram her. She is getting close, her walls are trying to cut off my cock. I bite down on her nipple as she lets out a scream. Fluids come gushing out of her as I lift her and push her back down, I can feel her juices dripping down my balls. I feel my balls tighten, and I know I am about to cum. With my thrusting faster I emptied inside her with her walls still tightened around I let her pussy milk me. I let her stay on the cock as she takes deep breaths. I look at her neck when my eyes see the vein in her neck. I couldn't help but start moving her gently on my cock.

Kris:"One more time baby, and you can rest "Closing my eyes I let the wolf take over. Through his eyes, I can see him licking and sucking on her neck while fucking her nice and slow. He bites down on her neck, and her walls tighten around him as he cums and locks into her, pushing the cum deeper into her womb. We lay there with my cock deep in her and I let her rest.

Coming out of the wolf haze, my cum is all over the snow at my feet. My cock rubbed raw and red. I can hear another bonded mate someplace in the woods giving out moans.

"I know, brother," I whisper. I know we have her now and we will never let go of her.

I make my way back to the cabin with a raw cock rubbing against my pants. Our wolves need our mate just as we do. If I would not look like I pissed my pants I would have put snow on my dick. We said we would wait until all her mates were here so we can all be with her and claim her. By the looks of it and the way, we all reacted and had to rush someplace else to get a release. I have a feeling we all will be deep in that pussy before the three numb nuts get home. I don't care they should have not been fucking idiots. I will make.sure to tell them all about being in our mates pussy. They will just have to get over it, they should not have left before Christmas week.


Jasper


Fuck, here I am out in the woods beating my dick cause my mate's pussy set my wolf off. Rubbing my pierced cock and pulling on the piercings to give me some pain. I can see her in front of me under the desk. Looking down at her mouth is open begging.
Emma:" Jasper, I am hungry".
Jasper:"You want this baby, finger your pussy while you suck on my cock."


Ghosted Black Ice By D.Chaney

I squeeze my cock harder as the cold reminds me of where I truly am. I look down at her face, and she licks her lips as she takes my cock into her mouth. She looks up at me and I can see in her face she is hungry for my cum, the devil's tongue she has. Her tongue snakes around my cock, my breath hitches as she rubs my balls. Looking at her as she has me in her mouth, I watch as she pops my cock away from her mouth.

She pulls my balls in her mouth, twirling her tongue around.

Jasper:"Fuck, baby, that feels so good."

Looking at her with my balls in her mouth, I swear, she just smirked at me with my balls in her mouth. Reaching down, I rub my hand along her face.

Jasper:"Such a good girl."

I wrap my hand around my cock and squeeze it, pushing the pre-cum to the tip. Emma drops my balls and latches onto my cock, moaning on my cock. I could feel it deep in my balls, I was about to cum.

Jasper:"Baby I am about to come, Do you want to eat it, baby."

She doesn't answer, she takes my cock all the way, tears running down her eyes as I move while running her tongue.

I grab her jaw," You are going to swallow."

She gives my balls a squeeze with her hand and I cum hard in her mouth, still pumping in her throat. I can feel her swallowing, I pop my cock free from her mouth and watch as she licks my cock clean.

I move my chair back "Know fuck yourself."

I watch her sit on her ass and spread her knees so I can see her nice wet pussy.

I can see drips dropping out of her two. I see her fingers sliding in a circle above her clit. She shifts her hips as she rubs her clit moaning with each rub. Her scent gets stronger as she is about to cum.

Jasper:"Does my mate like to suck cocks, good thing you have six of them ready and willing to be there to stuff that mouth. We will stuff that ass and pussy till you blackout with pleasure."

I watch as she keeps rubbing till she screams my name.

Coming to, there is cum all over my hand, wiping my hand in the snow. Pulling my pants up , the metal bars in my piercings are ice cold , it's making my cock hurt from being in the open cold for two long.

The hint of sweet apples is in the air, Kris was

around here someplace. Just realized I left Felix, Leo,

and Miles on video call since they could not be

there, we agreed we would do video chats so they

could be there somehow. Four days till Christmas,

we all hope they get home before then.

Chapter Eight - I hear people (4 Days )

Emma


I don't know how long I have been watching TV. I kept feeling like I was being watched, the guys have not come back, so I don't know why the feeling would not go away. Watching the team on the ghost show go through this abandoned building in the woods. The team leader leads the other members to one of the bedrooms, old wallpaper is falling off the wall, the glass paneling on the window has been broken and ivy has started to come through the window. With each step, there is a creaking sound shifting the floorboards. The wind was coming through the window moving the tattered curtains.

Stained with mold and yellow it floats in the air like an invisible ghost has picked it up. It stays that way for a while before I slowly lower it back to its place against the ivy. I don't know if they did see the curtain cause they looked like they were about to light some candles and have a seance with an Ouija board. Formed in a circle they stand in the middle of the room the leader pulls out a recorder and says silence. The leader took a deep breath before they spoke.

"Hello if you hear why don't you come and speak with us" the leader says.

There is a thump someplace in the house, and the team members scream running out of the room and

Ghosted Black Ice By D.Chaney

through the rest of the house. One of the cameramen trips on the way out and the camera crashes, causing a jump scare. Looking around I still have that feeling that I am being watched. Looking around again I don't see anyone. Since they are nowhere to be seen and I am thirsty I hope they don't mind me getting a glass of water. Throwing the blanket from my legs I get up from the lounge seat and make my way to the kitchen. That's when I see three faces on the laptop screen I make my way over to the computer screen. I give them a wave before I say something after a second they all point to their ears while saying I am muted. Looking at the computer screen I see the mute button on the laptop.

I click the button that unmutes these men.

Emma: "So one of you said something so I know I have unmuted myself."

They all rush at once.

Felix: "Hello beautiful, " the one with red hair said.

Miles: "Hello there darling" the blonde hair one said.

The third one opens and shuts his mouth.

Emma: " I am Emma, I don't know where the gentlemen who live here went."

Miles: "They will come back soon, why don't you sit down." the blonde one said.

I pull the stool back from the island and take a seat

The redhead waves at the screen

Emma: "I take it you three are the ones that love her with the others."

Leo: "You would be correct on that."

Felix: "Hello there Miss Emma my name is Felix."

Emma: "So you are the chef that I have heard some much about."

Felix: "Yes I am, I hope I make a flight back home soon so I can cook you a meal."

The one with the blonde hair speaks up again

Miles:" Hello there I am Miles and nice to meet you. I am a doctor and I would like to know how you are feeling today."

Emma: "I feel fine, thanks for asking. It's nice to meet you, Miles."

Leo: is there anything that you will need all you have to do is ask

Miles: if you start to feel off you just have one of the guys get in contact with me

Emma " Of course I will but I am sure I am fine."

Leo: "So how did you come to be in our home, Emma."

Emma: "It's a funny story. The snow was coming down heavily and I was in a complete whiteout. So I pulled off the side of the road and decided to take a breather since I was already freaking out. When I finally settled in the right mind I tried to pull onto the road again. With my luck, my car decided to die on me. With my phone being dead as well I decided to hunker down in my vehicle until help arrived. Then I woke up here in the cabin."

Leo: "Well I am glad you made it to our home safely."

I look at the guys and I can't read their expressions. Looking more in-depth it looks like the guys are in business suits and the background is in their hotel room.

Emma: " This is strange right or is it just me ."

They all give out a giggle shaking their heads. I never felt nervous in my life. I don't even know why well that's a lie I do know why social disorder.

Leo: "It's a little strange but once we know each other I am sure we will be laughed at in no time."

He is right once I am around them and see who they are, I will open up and be more myself. It takes a while and even though I am only here till the roads open up I wanted to stay longer I wanted to build something with these men. I don't know why but do I want to be a part of their lives maybe Nana was right I need some dick or what my head wants is six dicks cause these men are hot as fuck. My pussy is a hoe I know me and Frost had a moment earlier who said there will be anything with the others.

Felix:" Did the guys cook your food ."

I could not help but burst out laughing thinking about what the guys said this morning. Covering my mouth with my hand it's not that I am going to tell him that these friends said I cook better than him. The man is a chef.

Emma: "I cooked breakfast, I have issues with quirks. When I am in a new place I can't eat until I feel safe."

Felix: "Well I hope you are more comfortable when all gets come i can't wait to cook for you."

Looking at him I can see through the camera that my cheeks were beet red. Was it hot in here or is it just me?

I don't know how long the four of us talked but it felt like years. They had me laughing and crying with stories of Kris, Jasper, and Frost. I guess the six of

Ghosted Black Ice By D.Chaney

them grew up together and have been linked since birth. Leo said don't let leo mood wings bother me he is a real teddy bear at heart. They told me not to let Jasper's boyish charm make him look less like the man is a business. Which had me kinda scared since I have my learning issues.

Miles was in the middle of telling me how Frost peed the bed till he was seven. Because he was afraid of ladybugs. I was laughing so hard that when I finally looked back up, frost was standing behind me. He looks better than he did before.

Frost:" I see you have met the other guys."

Emma" Yeah they were sitting here all by themselves."

Felix: "What are the plans for today?"

Frost: Well I know Jasper was working on paperwork before he went to check the mail. Kris went to get wood, they should be back soon though. Emma and I were on the couch watching ghost shows."

Miles: "I have nothing to do today since there are no flights able to come into Ohio yet. If it's okay with you Emma can we just hang out ."

Leo: " Same here Miss Emma."

Felix: "It would be a pleasure to spend the day with you."

Ghosted Black Ice By D.Chaney

Instead of doing what they could in the hotels or the cities they were in they wanted to spend time with me. I can feel my cheeks getting warm.

Emma: " Sure why not, I just hope you all don't get bored."

Leo, Felix, Miles: "We won't!"

The door opens and Mr. Grump his hands are empty. He stops to take off his coat and his shoes. His arms look bigger than my waist out of the three of them he is the biggest. I want to snuggle him and have his arms wrapped around me. Fuck if I keep these thoughts going on in my head I will have to take a shower sooner then later. So I can get some pleasure. I want them all in my bed at the same time. Hell, I want them for life but I know I can't have them. I know me and frost had that moment. I don't know what is wrong with the first time in years I wanted a man or better six men in my life.

Emma: "Did you forget the wood?"

Kris aka Mr. Grump: "The wood was wet, very very wet."

He walks back over to the sink and starts doing the dishes again. I could not help but look at the other when they let out a giggle and shook their heads.

Miles: " I bet it was very very wet, I can't trust wood to stay dry and hard all the time."

I have a feeling we are not talking about wood.

Kris: "You all can shut the fuck up."

Ghosted Black Ice By D.Chaney

Frost comes to my side and places his hand on my back. I look up at his face, his blue eyes look brighter than before.

Frost: "Do you want to finish watching ghost shows before lunch or we can do something else."

Emma: "Yes I would love to finish off the ghost show."

I look back at the laptop. I can't just leave them here on the kitchen table.

Emma: "Would you three like to join us to watch ghost shows or would you like to do something else. '

Leo: "Go ahead and pick this us up and place us wherever we are not going any place."

I quickly unplug the computer and pull it to my chest. I walk back over to the lounge and place them at the foot. Facing them toward the TV and getting myself back into the seat. Frost takes his seat next to me. I can feel his body heat coming off his body. The door opens up and in walks Jasper his hair in disarray he stops and pulls his coat and shoes off. He has a smile on his face making his way back to where his laptop was before. Stopping when he saw that it was no longer there. I watch as he turns around and looks and turns around again. He looks down at the foot of the lounge and smiles as he

makes his way over to me. He plops down beside me.
He leans down his mouth and whispers in my ear.

Jasper: "You stole my laptop."

Emma: "You left your friends red and abandoned."

Jasper: "What do you want to have for lunch."

Popcorn is what gives butter and salt goodness. I
hope they have popcorn popping.

Emma "Popcorn with a lot of butter and salt."

Kris: " Do you want me to make it? Would you like to
make it?"

It must be something new because both Japer and Frost have a look of shock on their faces.

Emma: "If you five will excuse me."
I walk into the kitchen leaving the rest in the living room.

Emma: "Do you have popping popcorn and a pot with a lid."

Kris: " OF course we do. Do you want to watch me do it or do you want to do it?"

Emma: " I have perfected the art of popcorn making so I will make it."

Ghosted Black Ice By D.Chaney

I watch as he pulls the popcorn and the pot out and places it on the island near me.

Emma: "Would it be okay if I open the fridge and get some things."

Kris leans down to face me, his brown eyes meet mine.

Kris: " You can use whatever you want in this house, even Felix knives. No one will tell you no in this house ."

He leans down close to my ear. I can feel the puff of his breath hit my skin causing the hair on my arms to rise. I swear I can feel his lips on my ears.

Kris: "You tell me if someone tells you no while you are here and I will punch them in the face."

I can tell that he meant what he said. I don't know if his threat turns me on more or the fact that I want to see him punch someone in the face just not anyone who lives there.

I open the sleek modern built-in fridge pulling the butter from the fridge.

We were all sitting on the couch with our popcorn. Jasper and Frost were on either side of me and Kris was on down the coach. This paranormal team was out in the woods at the old abandoned farmhouse in one of the barns. The barns looked like they had seen better days; there were holes in the walls. They have their paranormal tools laid out trying to reach the old tobacco farmer. A loud growl can be heard and then the sound of someone scratching the side of the barn. The slamming of the barn door is what makes me jump inches off the coach.

Kris:" You never know when something will go bump in the night. "

He says in a loud boom scaring me inches off the couch.
Emma : " yea you never know what could be out in the dark."
Stuffing a handful of popcorn in my mouth

Kris comes into the bathroom deep inside. I didn't
and did want to ask if I could use the shower. Nana
popped in my head " now man wants a sinking pussy
and girl you are starting to smell.

Emma: " Do you think I could use the shower?"

Frost: "Of course you can take a shower if you need
to look in your bag for clothing over there on the
stool. If you need something warmer all you have to
do is ask."

Emma: " I am going to need something warmer."

I did need warmth but in reality I wanted all their
scents around me to smell so good.

All three of them get up and move from the couch
walking down the hallway where I see the main
bathroom is. I don't know what is in the other room
since the doors were closed. It was just me and the

three men on the laptop. Picking up the laptop and placing it on my knees. I hate that I am boring and I bet they wish they didn't have to put up with me. The three are great actors because I would not want to be on a live chat with a woman in my house just because.

Emma: "Have you heard anything about a flight home yet."

Leo: " No little darling, there has been no news about a way home."

Felix: " We are waiting on a phone call and as soon as the darn Dayton airports open we will be on the next flight."

Miles: "Well are all in the same boat, my little flower all on standby waiting on the airport to reopen.

One of the guys that went down down yelled out I couldn't tell who it was but what they said made me giggle.

" Tell those video chat boys you have to be done for the say and they can see you tomorrow cause you're getting in the bath soon."


Looking down at the computer I can see through the video feed that my eyes are wide. What the fuck do say to them. Telling them the truth I don't think I could lie to any of them.

Emma: " Look I hate to leave you guys but I need a bath or shower. It also looked like the three of you needed to get some sleep. I promise I will call you when I get up."

They did want to get going and if I am honest I

didn't want to let them go. I would be more than

happy to bring them into the bathroom with me but

the deep crest moons under their eyes I can tell they

need to get as much sleep. When I finally got them

off the computer and I shut the lid I felt it in my

body and soul. I missed them. I place the laptop on

the couch , reach down and pull the big manly socks

off my feet, rolling them into a sock ball to place

next to the laptop.


It was not looking before the guys walked back into

the room.

Kris came to me with a bundle of clothing. I can see

in the pile a big fluffy pair of sweatpants.

Jasper: " I am going to make something and bring it up to you while you are in the bath."

He steps back from the trio and makes his way to the kitchen. Looking back, Frost steps near me and leans down and picks up the abandoned laptop.

Frost: " I have some work I need to finish on the laptop. I will see you when you are done.

I watch as he turns and makes his way to the island. Kris steps forward with the bundle of clothing. Kris reaches his hand out and takes mine in his and pulls me off the coach. He pulls me down the hall and up a set of stairs and down a dark hallway. Big black french doors are opened to show an empty room. Kris pulls me into the room and I can see white all fucking white walls carpet. There is a door that must be a closet. Another door is slightly open; it looks

like there are flickering lights on. There is a
fireplace near the balcony doors. I could see it now
there is a deep black rug and me and the guys laying
in front of the fireplace cuddling.

Emma: " This is where you all kill me right."

Kris: " not funny princess ."

Emma: " Why is this room so empty ."

Kris: " That is a story for another time."

Pausing and letting my bare feet feel the plush
carpet. The smell of fresh paint and carpet still in
the air like this room was meant for some that has
not yet come.

Kris: " curious how would you do this room if it was
yours.

I look around the room and I know what I would do
with this room.

Emma: " I would paint the wall a dark blue almost black but not black. I would paint little gold metallic stars and moons on the walls, maybe even the zodiac.Black out curtains so the world doesn't see what I am doing. A big bed, dark blue bedding, all kinds of matching pillows. Tv on the opposite side of the bed so there person can watch tv. I would change the carpet to navy blue or black nothing white . Then again it is just my thoughts why do you ask.

Kris: " I am just wondering if women don't come here and I want to see how you would do in this room. If you have not noticed, we like four white walls and basic things."

Emma: " Yea it is pretty plan if you ask me and you did so that is what i would do with this room. Then again I live in a basement with my parents.

Ghosted Black Ice By D.Chaney

Kris: " you live in a basement that is strange and how old are you to live with your parents."

 I smack his chest and give them a grumpy dick my serious face.

Emma: " for your information I choose to live there. I live there to spend time with my nana.

Kris: " We will discuss this more later."

Kris grabs my arm and pulls me to the open door with the flickering lights.

Emma: " I am still waiting on you all to kill me."

Kris: " Again that is not funny."

Kris opens the door wider and I see the flickering light is a big tub with shelving around the tub. White candles in a U form flickering , looking down I see the tub have a mountain of bubbles, the scent of lavender and eucalyptus is in the air.There is a big window in the back wall you can see out the window. The room was breathed taking a big glass shower can be seen above the candle. The room was massive. I can't believe the guys don't use this room.

Kris: "How would you do this room for educational purposes."

Ghosted Black Ice By D.Chaney

Emma: "I would paint the walls as the foggy woods. Vines around the mirror to give off the mother nature vibe."

Kris looks around the room almost like he is trying to picture what I pictured.

Kris: " well i will let you get a bath and private time. If you need anything just yell out and someone will be here to help."

He looks around the room again, then he walks out. I guess everything was perfect. Looking around the room I could really see the room.
Maybe one day I will have those rooms I always wanted to have.

## Chapter Nine- Cumming in the bathroom

Jasper

We all decided while we were pulling clothing from each of our rooms that I would cook her food and take it to her and Frost would finish off the paperwork since he could get it done fast. Not like me but better than Kris who hates electronics. I pulled the beef stew out from the fridge and ladled some into bowls so we could eat.

I was placing the food on the tray, so I could not take it up to her while she was in the bath. Kris stayed upstairs in the mate suite to make sure she was okay. In case she needed something, he would be there for her when she yelled out. Kris had a hard life. His parents did the unthinkable to him that why he closed off, I never thought he would show such emotion to our mate as he already has. She has truly changed her life for the better, and I hope she realizes she has all six of us to love her and cherish her till the end of time.

I was about to ask Frost if he thinks I should take her soup up now but that is when I smelt it her pussy was calling to me. I could not stop myself as I walked toward the stairs.

Kris

I was in the mate library with the door open so I could hear her call out to me if she needed me. I would be there in a heartbeat. I can't say how much finding her means to me cause it means more than the world to me that she is finally here. I did have a good life. My parents left me at a gas station. Maybe in their final attempt to save me in their drug filled mind. The abuse and pain that they caused would have me run from foster home and make my way back to that gas station sitting on the side of the building waiting for them to come back for me. They never did and when the cops started getting called when the gas station clerk saw me that was when I knew there was no love in the world. I hated the world and everyone on it. By luck a kind couple adopted me and took me into their home. That's

Ghosted Black Ice By D.Chaney

when my life changed. I met my bonded brothers and we have been connected at the hip since all six of us.

Looking out the windows the snow is coming down again. Four days till Christmas and it will be the first one with our mate. I can't wait till the others in the group chat on how she wants her room and bathroom.

We are going to have to order a big bed or hire someone to make an eight person bed cause we all need room.

She has a smart mouth on her and I can't wait to smack the perky ass someday soon. Been her over my knee and made those cheeks red. I was about to slip into a sex dream when I smelt her chocolate strawberries faint but I know her body is calling mine. Like a moth to the flame I follow the scent

back to her bathroom.


Frost

I was working on the paperwork, and seeing all

Kris's mishaps and misspellings gave me a chuckle.

He really hates computers. He even said, so I ate this

mother fucking computers. Jasper was warming up

the soup and Kris was up there with Emma just in

case she needed one of us. I know she likes us all,

and I know she is worried about being with us. What

she doesn't know is that times have changed and

people are more welcome to a woman being loved by

more than one man. Hell, the times have changed

there are tons of books out there with why to choose

and reverse harems. Who we love or how many we

love don't change who we are as a person. Filing the report into the backup system on our business drivers. I was about to go shopping for our mate when I smelled she was in need. She is calling me.

Emma

I watch as he walks out of the bathroom and turns the corner, and I step out into the blank room. He is truly gone, looking around. I have so many questions on why they have an empty room. I will ask questions later. Those bubbles are calling names, pulling down my pants along with my underwear and kicking them to the side. Lifting the hem of my shirt over my head, dropping it down on the floor so

I can take my bro all. Bending down, I pick up my clothes and place them on the counter, so I can maybe wash them or not. The scents of the essential oils are soothing to me. Stepping into the warm bubbled water, the bubbles pop and let out little foamy sounds as they surround my feet and legs. Sitting down in the warm water, I let the heat settle to me. Nana always pops into my head. She always said if you are sick take a bath if you are sad take a bath, she claimed it washes whatever the problem away.

I could always imagine what I look like at the moment. Laughing in my head, I am a hot damn mess. I have fallen for six men. I would keep them forever if I could. Taking the washcloth and the soap

Ghosted Black Ice By D.Chaney

that they have laid out, how did they know I like these scents? Lavender is my favorite. Closing my eyes, I run the washcloth down my thigh. I don't know the fact that I am in the house with all these men, but my body tingles and my clit pulsates when I run the cloth on my skin. Dropping the washcloth in the water some place. I run my index finger and middle finger down the middle of my pussy lips. I swear I can feel my clit move with my heartbeat. I rub my two fingers around my clit. The feeling is so good. I couldn't help but think of having all three of the men at once, Two in my mouth, one in each hand and two in my tight pussy. My nipples were and wanting to be sucked they ached . I could see one of the men taking one of my nipples in their mouth. Rubbing faster on my clit I know that I am close to cumming. I can feel it all over my body. The built up pressure was going to give me a sex high and I needed to be on one if I was going to be around these men. Moaning out loud it doesn't take long and my body shakes and I can feel a cold liquid jet out of me as i cum. I keep rubbing and pushing my body to let more of my realse out. My body shakes, unable to control it . My clit is super sensitive and she is still throbbing for need.My arms and body are heavy and I drop them to my side and let them relax once more. Closing my eyes I take in the rich lavender scent.

I don't know how long my eyes are closed but I swear I could hear footsteps in the bedroom.

The again I i could be my imagination or my pussy hoping the guys are coming to fill her with there cocks. I was about to run my fingers on my clit again when I felt someone was touching me, any place else I would have scream and fought. Since I was in this house with three men, I knew it had to be one of them. With great effort, I open my eyes half way to see that it is Kris on his knees with his hand in the water. I can feel his thumb and index finger rolling and squeezing my nipple. All I could do was arch my back and moan out in pleasure. Looking at Kris, there are no words that need to be said. It was like we could read each other and what each other needed. Looking into his eyes, I can see that his pupils are blown and he is hungry. There was no ring of brown in his brown eyes.

Kris kept rolling my nipple in his finger and I
continued to look at him. His jaw was tight. I lift my
hand up to his hand that is in the water  and move to
grab his wrist. I pull his hand down my stomach to
the top of my pussy, never breaking eye contact with
kris. I let go of his wrist and went to where his hand
was before I took control. I pinch my own nipples
and let out a moan of pleasure.

He has yet to touch me, thinking I read the
situations wrong. I was about to apologize when I
felt the tips of his finger feather on my at the
opening of my pussy lips. He takes his finger down
and rubs my clit then moves on down to my pussy
hole two fingers enter me and circle the tip of

Ghosted Black Ice By D.Chaney

entrance. Then he would move them back up and do it all over again. Why is this turning me on so much? My breath keeps catching with every swipe of his fingers. I wanted to taste him and I planned to.

Breaking eye contact with Kris, my eyes go low to his sweatpants. The huge bulge can be seen on the outline of his cock. Licking my lips and looking back up to his eyes without saying a word, I know what he wants and I know that he knows what I am about to do. With much will power I pull myself away from his gliding hands. I move to my knees in the tub letting the bubble coat me like a blanket, looking into his eyes I blindly reach out and hook my fingers at the elastic of his sweat pants not caring about the water drops i am leaving on his pants. I pull them down freeing his cock, of course the grump is not

wearing any boxers. I should be shocked by that, but

not. What shocked me was the smiley tattoo, a round

yellow dot with a black ring around the yellow circle

with a smile on its face.

Now I will not snort. Why the hell would he place it

on his pelvic bone if the owner is happy or is the

cock happy, or both. I took a deep breath and I could

not hold it in any longer, I let out a giggle, should I

call his cock Mr. happy. Maybe another time, me and

Mr. happy can have some private time while put duct

tape it over his mouth shut.

His cock springs out to meet me, what a greeting,

looking back up to his eyes, We don't have to say a

thing, his eyes are telling me everything I need to

know. He wants this as much as I do or more mixed

Ghosted Black Ice By D.Chaney

with love and pain. Deep down, I do feel that way for all of them.

Reaching out to keep my focus on him, I stroke his cock, cupping the end of each movement. Breaking eyes with him, I lean over and lick his balls. Sucking both of his balls in my mouth, I wiggle my tongue around until I find what he likes, the figure of weight all over his balls. I hear a growl sound above it that almost sounds like an animal. The growl broke into a moan. I was close to thinking he was growling mad that I was sucking on his balls. Letting his balls fall out of my mouth, I work my tongues on the base of his, cocksucking on the underneath. I work my way slowly up a little, then back down till I reach the tip of his cock. I suction my mouth over his cock and I can hear him take a deep breath. I take him deep down my throat, flicking my tongue in a u formation around his cock. I move my head back and forth. Slurping and moans have my pussy throbbing to be fucked.

I wanted to swallow all his cum to feel my belly full. He grunts and starts to move faster in my mouth. With one hand, I grab his ball and give them a squeeze. His moans get louder, wrapping my arm around his back to grab his butt cheek.

His hand comes down on my head and his fingers tangle with my hair. He pulls my hair and with the pain I moan around his cock. His pace gets faster, and I can tell that he will be coming soon. Thanks to the devil I am in the water or there would be a puddle all over the place. I don't know why, but the sound of a moan always did it for me and had me cumming in seconds. I dig my nails into his ass, his movement falters, and he moans louder, his cock jerks. I can feel his jets of cum run down my throat, letting it run down my throat as I continue to work his cock. I suck and swallow all the cum. Pulling away, I lick his cock clean and sucking his balls clean. They're less full than they were before, but his cock wanted more, and so do i.

Looking up, I lick my lips, this motherfucker has a smirk on his face. Without a hello or a fuck you, he bends over and picks me up like a rag doll and sit me down on the wide tub ledge. There was no time to recover Kris as my legs spread wide, water dripping all over the place. I watch as he stands back up and finishes pulling his pants off his body. I watch as he gets down on his knees and runs those fingers through my pussy lips again. Rubbing my clit for a little bit before he makes his way to my pussy hole. I watch as his arm reaches over and snatches a candlestick from the glass holder.

The candle is still going strong, fluttering and dancing. Kris tilts the candle he starts at the middle of my thighs moving to where he now has my pussy lips spread open he hovers. The candlestick, letting the drops of candle ways drop on my pussy lips and over my clit. My breath hitches and it takes all of my will power not to cum with the pain. He then moves the candle to my other thigh. He trails the candlestick back over, spreading my pussy lips open to let the wax pour down my pussy. Gripping the ledge I move my body forward. I want this pain with his cock. When he is done pouring the wax all over my pussy he starts to move up my body across my stomach the drops let tingle as they hit my flesh heat and lust that is what I am feeling. He goes all the way between my breasts before he moves to my right breast. Kris circles my nipple with the candle, letting the drops fall on my hardened peak and around. Fuck I need this man to fuck me already he moves to my other breast doing the same thing letting the drop coat my harden peaks.

I close my eyes, trying to keep from cumming all over the place. Trying to calm myself to think about things that will make you less horny milk , that woman at the store the other day when I was getting cookie supplies that smelled like rotten tuna fish.

Yep, that did nothing better to kill a pussy boner

than thinking of rotten pussy.

The hint of smoke touches my nose, opening my

eyes I see that Kris has blown out the candle again,

this motherfucker has a smirk on his face. I watch as

the candle go lower, watching as he takes his hand

and spread my pussy lips, the wax is falling on the

tile tub edge. Kris takes the end of the candle and

rubs the candlestick over my clit, up and downside

to side. His other hand goes down to my pussy hole

and inserts two fingers, stretching me as he works

the candle sick on my clit.

Wct sounds are coming from my pussy, Kris pulls the

candlestick from my pussy. I watch as he pushes the

candlestick in my pussy while his fingers are still in

my pussy stretching me. He pushes the candle further and further inside of me. Where the fuck did they find these long as candle sticks.

Kris: " I can't wait to do the same to that perky little ass and asshole, will you scream as I drop wax on the puckered hole."

I can tell that I was about to cum all over the place. I reach back, bracing my hands on the edge of the ledge. Kris pulls his finger from my pussy hole, Kris wraps his hand around my tight to pull my body closer to him. He pushes his face into my pussy and licks the and sucks the wax off my pussy. The candle is still going in and out of my pussy, my hip in motion with the candlestick.

Emma: "I am about to cum."

I moan out as I close my eyes, his teeth scraping on my sensitive flesh, and I am cuming all over the place. Not wanting to look and see his face as my fluids coat his face and body. When my body finally stops shaking, I open my eyes and realize we are no longer alone in the bathroom.

Ghosted Black Ice By D.Chaney

Chapter Ten - Let's Make A Splash

Emma

Looking at the other two men, who have now joined us in the bathroom. Jasper and Forest are on either side of Kris, I watch as Kris hands the candlestick over to Frost's open hand. Frost grabs the dripping-wet candlestick. I don't know what he plans to do with the candlestick, but I am already turned again.

I watch as Frost takes the candlestick and bring it to his nose and give it a deep inhale. I watch as he takes the candlestick from his nose and brings it lower to his mouth. He gives me a smirk and then sticks his tongue out and licks the candlestick. Frost closes his eyes and opens his mouth and sticks the candlestick in his mouth and moans around the candlestick. The moans keep escaping his mouth. Fuck, that was hot, the throbbing in my clit is back and more intense than before. My pussy is clinching with need and I have a heartbeat deep in my pussy, and she wants a dick. I can feel my excitement dripping down my ass crack. Jasper leans forward, running his fingers in my juices before he stuffs them in my mouth. Kris leans forward and does the same, but he sticks his finger in his own mouth, letting out a moan.

Ghosted Black Ice By D.Chaney

Frost: "Our girl tastes so delicious, Strawberries and chocolate."

He moans as he continues to lick the candle clean.

Jasper went to get more of my juices on his finger and started pouting.

Jasper: " Kris you asshole you took it all what the fuck."

Jasper looks over to Frost with a pout .


Jasper: " You could have shared the juice's Frost."

Looking at Jasper, I see that he has started to strip his sweatpants and boxer off his body.

 but

Japer: " You might have gotten her sweet nectar, I will be in that pussy first."

I watch as this man bounces on his feet and rubs his hands together. I could not help but glance down as his cock bounced with him like it is happy to be freed from its cage. The tip of his cock was white cream dripping out of the slit at the top. I didn't expect there to be a piercing on his cock and to be honest I am turned the fuck on. I watch as he takes a step closer to me and reaches out and grabs my arms and pulls me to my shaking legs, Kris reaches out and grabs my hips keeping me up right . Kris pulls me closer, and I can get Jasper sliding in behind my body. Another set of hands come down on my hips, pulling me back. I am slammed down on Jasper's lap. His cock is at my back, hard and ready. I can feel one of his hands start to leave my hip and trail over to my stomach, his fingertips feather on my skin. He continues to move his feathered touch along my skin. His fingers get lower and lower as they make contact with my pussy lips. Unlike Kris, he uses the tips of three fingers and rubs circles on my very sensitive clit. I could not help but buck under his touch. I could not go far because his other hand kept me in place. I watch as Frost places the candle down beside the lit candles. He steps Closer to me, he reaches out, and I think he is about to embrace my face, but I was wrong. His hand wraps around my throat, his thumb moving back and forth. He leans down, his face inches from mine.

Frost:"Is your clit sore, baby."

Shaking my head yes because it is and at the same time it is not is throbbing. I can't speak because Jasper fingers are working so hard to keep me from talking and the fact that he is also grinding his cock against my butt cheek . Kris squeezed my neck to bring me back to focus.

Kris:" Good, it's going to be really sore because this pussy is ours."

A warm breath comes across my ear.
Jasper:" We are going to ruin your tight little pussy for anyone else. This pussy belongs to all six of us, we own this clit this hole and that tight asshole baby, understand."

Ghosted Black Ice By D.Chaney

Shaking my head yes, cause in the end I want to be owned by these six men.

Frost tightens his hand on my throat and brings his thumb on my chin.

Frost:" Do you really understand, Emma, you belong to us as we belong to you."

Kris spreads my legs so they're draped over Jasper's . Jasper removes his hand from my pussy. Lifts me up and moves his cock from rubbing my ass to having it rubbing my pussy lips. I can feel each one of Jasper's pricing as they move against me. Jasper keeps motion and grinds into me. Frost still didn't take his pants off, his hand still wrapped around my throat. Kris leans forward and runs his tongue over my lips, when he pulls back I see his hand is dripping wet bubbles on his hand. I watch as he wraps his hand around his cock, moving up and down, cupping his head and back down. Watching for a few seconds before I look back at Frost, his hand on my neck. The three are working together to get release and to give me my own . Reaching out to Frost, I run my hands out along the front of his pants, I can feel the bulge hard as a rock. He tightens his hand around my neck, and I move up to push my hand down his pants. I feel the wetness on his pants from his pre-cum. Jasper's fingers trail down my body. He reaches my clit, gives it a quick rub as he still rubs his pierced cock . He pushes two fingers into me with each thrust in and out, he slowly spreads his fingers with every thrust of fingers.

Ghosted Black Ice By D.Chaney

Kris: " Do you think you can take Jasper's fingers along with his cock.

Without a sound to understand what the fuck was even said. Jasper is slamming inside of me, filling me with both his cock and his finger, stretching me. Stretching me, the pain becomes pleasure and I want more. I can feel his piercings hitting all the best spots, fuck, I am going to be addicted to this.

Emma: " Oh god, fuck , feels so good."

My pussy is milking Jasper's finger and cock, she wanted more. My pussy was a fool on whores mission, she wanted all the cocks.

With Kris in front of me working his cock and my hand still wrapped around Frost cock. How many hands does Jasper have, because I feel fingers on my clit. Breathing out "I am about to cum" I couldn't take it anymore, the pressure was building and building. As jasper continues to fuck me with his cock and all the fucking fingers. Frost put his hand on the back of my head and makes my me go forward.

Frost:" You will not cum yet, Emma, we all will cum together."

I clench my pussy around, Jasper moans in my ear, he thrust deeper into my pussy. This was going to be hard not to come before them guys. I am already there, ready to let my body take over. .

Ghosted Black Ice By D.Chaney

I couldn't help but close my eyes, thinking unsavory thoughts to keep my body under control. Frost pulls my head back by my hair, and the pain makes me moan out loud . Looking at Frost in the eyes and his eyes hold  the wickedness in them.

Frost: " Be a dear and suck on Kris' cock ."

I look over to Kris, who has his cock in his hand, rubbing back and forth to the head and down to the base.

I lean forward as Kris steps closer. He takes the head of his cock and rubs it over my lips, painting my lips with his precum.

I part my lips and suck him into my mouth he moves closer to me moving my tongue under his cock. I take his cock down my throat, and I feel a hand on my throat, closing my airway. I reach out to Frost and move my hand up and down and his cock. I was going to explode soon if these men did not cum soon.

Jasper:"I am about to cum baby and I am going to fill this pussy with my cum."

Frost:"I am going to cum princess all over this hand."

Kris: " Just like before, I am going to jet my cum down to that belly."

My vision was starting to go black when I felt his cock flex in my mouth. Kris lets out a loud groan, and I feel his warm cum run down my throat again. Not soon after that, my hand on Frost cock twitches and his hand tightens around my throat as warm wet jets coat my hand. Blackness and dots coat my vision, and I feel like I am floating into the darkness.

Jasper fucks me harder, and I hear him grunt and moan, his cock flexes inside my pussy and I squeeze him and his fucking fingers. " My pussy" Jasper grunts out, and I let loose and cum so hard I push off Jasper and watch as a fountain shouts out of me.

Chapter Eleven- Let's wet some sheets

Emma

My body shook all over. I had no handle on my movement. Kris came in front of me, placing his hand on my chest. Jasper wrapped his arms around my body, both working to keep me from falling to the floor.

Good thing, because I am sure Kris's cock would have impaled me in the eye. How did I get a black eye? I got a cock to the face. I could not help but let out a little giggle as my body calmed down.

Japer: "What a funny little girl."

Ghosted Black Ice By D.Chaney

He asked me while rubbing my side and giving my back kisses.

Emma: " It's nothing." I say leaning my head back on Jasper's body.i sure the fuck didn't want to tell them about cock to the eye.

Jasper:' Well, tell us anyway ."

Emma: " Well, I was thinking how funny it would be if I got a black eye 'cause I leaned forward and dick to the eye."

Kris: "That would not be funny at all."

Frost: " I mean, it would be a little funny to watch her tell people how she got the black eye."

"This pussy was amazing and wrapped my cock so well" Jasper He kissed the side of my face

Frost: " How about you and Jasper finish with your bath? Kris and I will make up the bed so we can all go to sleep."

It is like he knew what I was going to say next. I mean, I have no issues with sleeping on the couch.

Frost: " No you will not sleep on the couch."

They didn't even give me the time to just walk out the room. Standing up, I turn around as Jasper is already sanding and is now facing the tub. I was as he steps into the tub and lowers his body , I continue to watch him as he sits down and leans back.

Jasper: " Now come on and join me, baby, let me rub your back."

He reaches his hand out for me to grab his hand . I try to look where I am stepping, nothing like a miss-step, and ends up with my foot on his cock.

I step between his legs, turn my back to him and grab the edges of the tub, placing my but above his cock. I did say that my pussy is a cock hungry bitch. I lean back on his chest. He grabs the abandoned wash cloth and pours some soap on and squeezes the cloth till it's full of foam. I close my eyes and just take at this moment, a man willing to take care of me. This was new to me. I never had to happen before with a man. He's washing me as gently as can be. I hope he knows this moment means so much to me.

Japer: " Put your feet up on the ledge and scoot down. I want to wash your hair and snuggle you before we go to the bedroom"

I do as he asks. I scoot myself down his body and realize his cock is inches from the side of my face. I turned my face and kissed the side of his dick, letting him know this moment matters to me. The sound of a bottle being open and the suction sounds. One of his hands comes down in my head and his fingers do little circles. His other hand comes down, moving the running soapy suds down my hair.

Jasper: "Don't feel ashamed about wanting us all. We want you two, all of you the good and the bad and when I mean all of us I mean all six "Jasper says, and I am shocked that they want me in this short amount of time. Because this has a time limit for all of us, when the time runs out I will be a ghost in the wind, and it would be better that way.

Jasper: "You ready, baby girl."

Ready for what his cock, the other cocks what should I be ready for. What the hell, you only live once, I will take a chance.

Emma: "Sure, yea, I am ready."
I said, watching as he turned a knob by the faucet. It takes a few seconds, but little cold droplets come down from the ceiling. Jasper rubs both hands in my hair and I close my listening to the water come down like rain and each drop hits my skin. The feel of hands rubbing threw my hair in my scalp.

Jasper

As I rub my hands through my mate's hair. I watch her breast move up and down. I know she is sleepy as her chest slows and her mouth parts open. I watch her as I clean her skin off. Taking care of our mate is our job . I flick off all the way that is on her belly and up her breast. Who knew she liked wax play and the way Frost choked her while she had Kris cock in her mouth. She is perfect for us. She is going to give us hell. She took us all like a champ. The only problem is I don't know how I am going to get her out of the tub. I was lucky that Kris decided to walk in still naked, but so am I. Whispering to him to clean her pussy since I can't reach her there. He shakes his head and reaches his hand out. Handing him the wash cloth, I watch as he spreads her open and wipe her clean, she moans as the wash cloth comes across her clit. He takes the wash cloth and rings it out before placing it on the sink.

He goes to walk out of the room I make. A sound stopping him in his tracks. He turns to look at me and I whisper to him to take her to the bedroom where she is going to sleep. He bent down and placed his arm under the neck and her bent legs. He heaves her up and walks out of the room. I make quick work getting up and pulling the plug on the tub. Blowing out the candles, I throw her wash cloth and clothing down the laundry shoot. Turning off the lights to make way to the Frost room. Leaving the mate suite for now, but we will soon have her there sleeping with us all every day. I can't wait to find out what she wants her room to be like.

She is going to be the most spoiled mate ever. We have worked hard for this day, and we all have saved for this moment. Hell we all could retire today and have money for a lifetime or many lifetimes.

Kris

I carried her to the Frost bedroom, and we collected blankets and pillows from each of her mates' rooms. We promised the other bonds that were away that we would have her laying down in the mixture of their scent. Frost was downstairs getting the stray food to bring it up so she can eat. I plop her down on the bed. Her nipples could have been hard from the cold air or lust. Frost lit the fire earlier while we were getting things set up , the cracking of burning wood made the room much calmer. I watch as my girl sleeps well, not my girl out girl . She won't be sleeping much longer, though Frost plans to eat her out. He said something about wanting to swallow her juices.He said when he gets back, he is going to wake her up with his tongue in her pussy. That there was no lying, she was going to ride his face.


Frost

I carry the tray of food as I make it back to my room. As I enter, I see Emma laid out on the bed like a starfish, placing the tray down on the dresser. Kris is sitting against my pillows and his naked ass is on my comforter. He better not fart on my blanket. Jasper has yet to join us, but I am not waiting on the man. He got to give her a bath, and I am a little jealous he got to wash her perky nipples and run his hands in her long black hair. We might have to build another room just for us all to be able to get into a bath with her. A custom-built tub so the seven of us can fit. So the six of her mates worship and bathe her.

I move to the bed and lean down. I whisper in her ear.

Frost: "Little mate, it's time to wake up and stop dreaming of our cocks, you dirty little girl."

She moves to lay in her stomach, clearly still asleep, and groans out.

Emma:"No, I have no appointments today so let me sleep in. She stuck her hand under her body to get them warm.


Frost: "Left to your knees and spread your legs."

Even in her sleep, she does what she is asked to. I watch as she struggles to get to her knees, since she was so close to the end of the bed that she keeps on flattening on the bed. After a few seconds she is still steady in and out of the dream world.  I sat down at the end of the bed. I leaned my head back on the bed, looking up at her flushed pussy. Her pussy hovers over my face. I blow on the lips of her pussy and watch as her hips move back and forth. The water from her bath drips around my head.

Frost: "Lay down, little mate."

She clearly didn't know I was here, because her pussy slams down on my face and my nose deep in her pussy. I take a lick along the valley, her pussy hole to her clit. Wrapping my arms around her hips to secure her to my face. I bite down on her clit and she moans out, and I can feel her trying to escape my mouth. She tried hard to pull her pussy away from me. I keep her in place and keep licking and biting.

Emma: " Fucking ,dam, shit eat me."

Sucking her swollen clit and flicking my tongue on her clit in my mouth. I keep sucking her clit. I feel her move above me as her body shifts. Instead of laying down, she is sitting on my face. She is running her fingers through my hair, tugging my hair as I suck and move my tongue and suck harder, removing by hand from keeping her caged. I trail my hand down her butt, I stop at her puckered hole. I take my finger and swirl it around the closed off hole that I plan to fuck very soon. Her moans get louder, and I push the tip of my finger in her puckered hole.

Emma: "Fuck, Frost, I am about to cum. Fuck, baby, keep sucking me."

Cum she does, she pours for me, her body shaking. My mouth is full and I swallow it all. My face is covered with her juices and I love it. Letting her go and watching her lift off my face, I move from being underneath her getting to my feet, letting her release drip down my face and onto my chest. I watch as she crawls up the bed and climbs on top Kris before she lowers her dripping pussy on his cock. I watched as Kris' head fell back to the headboard.

Kris: " Fuck princess, this pussy is so good."

Ghosted Black Ice By D.Chaney

I watch as she moves her hips. Her long black hair is like noodles, clingy to her flesh. I move to the side of the bed to get the site of her breast jiggle as she rides Kris cock. I break away from watching to see if Jasper has made it into the room. I look around, and I see he is sitting in the chair by the fireplace. I look over to the side of bed and watch Kris and Emma fuck. I get up from the bed and make my way over to the other chair by the fireplace, sitting down . I watch our mate continue to rise, Kris. The sound of slapping skin gets louder and bother, Kris and Emma's moans get louder and louder. Jasper and I watch as our girl cums all over Kris cock.

Jasper

I watch as she falls to the side of Kris. I stand up from my chair and make my way to the bed.

Japer: ' Come bring that pussy over here on your hands and knees."

I know she thought we were done with her, and she was so wrong.

Jasper: "Did you think this pussy was done, not by a long shot."

She crawls to the end of the bed and turns around, her pussy right in front of me. I could see Kris cum drops from her pussy onto the bed. I stop, a drop of cum and push it back into her. I don't ask if she was

Ghosted Black Ice By D.Chaney

on birth control. I don't really care the thought of one of us getting her pregnant, her belly swelling with a life being created. The mirror thought of us being a daddy to Emma baby and her growing belly. The thought of her pregnant does something to make my wolf more primal . I watch as Frost comes with the tray of food and sits on the side of the bed in front of us.

Frost: " While Jasper fucks you, I am going to feed you."


I watch as he loads the fork up and feeds, and while she is chewing, I slowly push my pierced cock into her pussy cum filled pussy. She moans, and she is wet with Kris cum and her own. That doesn't stop her tight pussy squeezing the cock.  The cum she had in her was coating my balls, dripping down between my legs. I slow down when Frost holds a fork to her mouth. After she takes a few more bites, I grab her hair a slam hard and fast into her pussy. My balls tighten, and I know I am to cum I feel her tighten around me and screams out and my cum hard filling her pussy and fucking my cum deeper into her. I let her loose and let her fall to the bed. Kris grabs a pillow and Frost turns her over and places her head down on the pillow, Kris continues to feed her one spoonful at a time.

Frost: " Eat up little girl, you're going to need your energy. We are not even close to being done, and we are still in round one."

Ghosted Black Ice By D.Chaney

Chapter twelve - group text and stop having sex (3 days)

Jasper

I am standing at the doorway watching my brothers and our mate cuddle in the bed. She is lying on Kris' chest with frost cuddling behind her. Kris has a hand on her back, keeping her close to his chest. I never thought I would see Kris like this. She has already started to change all of us. Never have I seen Kris this way. She has to be tired because after two more rounds and being fed by Frost while I was fucking her pussy. She was tired before we started fucking her, she has to be dead to the world to know.

After our mate fell asleep, the three of us chatted. Kris was telling us how she would like to do her room. Well, the room that she doesn't know is hers. I decided to stay awake while the others slept, so I could make a list and order things for her room. I pull my phone out of my pocket and take a few pictures of her sleeping. With one final look at her and my brothers, I leave them. Walking down the hall to my room.

Sitting down at my desk, I pull out my laptop. I didn't need to use the monitors but still, I looked over the screen checking the security cameras. The front, sides, and back of the house look good.

Focusing back on the laptop, I opened up multiple

shopping sites and set up a group text.


Emma'sHauntingHomies6

Invite sent to Leo

Invite sent to Miles

Invite sent to Felix

Invite sent to Kris

Invite sent to Frost


Leo accepted invite

Miles accepted invite

Felix accepted invite


Leo changed name to VampLeoDen

Miles changed name to witchdoc

Felix changed name to hornychef

Geekywolf - hornychef really Felix

Hornychef- yes really, what's going on

Geekywolf- we showed her her room well  Kris sorta ask her opinion on how she would decorate, so I am about to online shop and wanted to make us all a group chat

Witchdoc- well what does she want, we all can shop for her

Geekywolf- Kris said she would paint the bedroom a deep dark blue and paint gold stars and moons, so a celestial-themed room. Hold on, I will make a list of the things she mentions.

Hornychef- okay

Geekywolf-

paint the walls dark blue

gold stars and moon painted on the wall

black out curtains

dark blue bedding

pillows matching all kinds of pillows

change carpet dark blue and black

VampLeoDen - I will work on bedding, curtains, rug, and pillows

Hornychef- I will order the paint and carpet and stencils of moons and stars

Witchdoc- I am going to order her clothing, shoes, purses, and some jewelry

Geekywolf- I guess I will order stuff for her bathroom

VampLeoDen- I also am going to order books for her library and a TV for her room

Witchdoc-give us a list for the bathroom as well

Honeychef- yea bro we all have nothing to do till the airport open so send us a list

Ghosted Black Ice By D.Chaney

Geekywolf- she didn't say much about the bedroom

Foggy wood mural themed

vines wrapped around the mirror


VampLeoDen- I will look into the mural


Witchdoc- I will order vines and get plants to hang. I know the ones that will thrive in bathroom environment, I am also going to look for ideals on that pin site


VampLeoDen- I found a moon and stars that throw blankets that are reversible. I also found some hanging stars.

Geekywolf- From what Kris said, she is also likes the scent of lavender and eucalyptus bath soaps

VampLeoDen- What is she doing at the moment

Geekywolf- She is asleep between Kris and Frost

Witchdoc- Is she dressed

Geekywolf- Well no

Hornychef- we said we were all going to wait for when all of us can be with her


Geekywolf- Well, that was the plan, but we smelt her, and we could not stop our wolves wanted her pussy man can't help it

Witchdoc- well, at least it was just the one-time

Geckywolf- well it was not the one time it was a lot of times

VampLeoDen- Stop fucking our mate


Ghosted Black Ice By D.Chaney

Geekywolf- We can't help it, she smells so good and taste as good

Hornychef- this is complete bull shit

VampDenLeo- agreed, we had a plan to wait. I have been jacking my dick since I saw her on camera. You are all at the house are fucking her

Geekywolf- dude, she is a squirter

Witchdoc- fuck you three

Geekywolf - You all will be home soon, and then we all can be with her

VampLeoDen- Let's change the subject

Hornychef- besides fucking her, what are the plans for today.

Geekywolf- Well I planned on making cookies with her after they sleep get some sleep maybe go out and play in the snow

Hornychef- Well that sounds fun to make sure you all take pictures of all this

Geekywolf- sent a photo

Witchdoc- I could have done without seeing deflated cock

VampLepDen - I second that

Horneychef- you are all missing that point Kris is cuddling her, look at this body languages

Geekywolf- Sent a photo

Hornychef- Did you just blow up Kris deflated dick and sent it to us all he will kill you when he sees this you're going to have to buy him a new phone

VampLeoDen- Well I am ordering things for her room, and they will be there after the new years

Hornychef- What kind of cookies will you be making, do I need to send you some recipes

Ghosted Black Ice By D.Chaney

Geekywolf- No, we don't want a complete recipe
that take three hours

Witchdoc- how is she feeling, is she showing signs
of getting sick

Geekywolf- No, she is fine

VampLeoDen- Well let's order things for our mate,
we can chat later

Hornywolf- I agree, I am going to go look for crystals

Witchdoc-okay will talk later, I have one thing two
say to you Frost and Kris fuck you for fucking our
mate without us.

I lay my phone down on the desk and open another
web browser. I wanted to get her a few essential oil
diffusers for her bedroom and for around the house.
I also wanted to get her bedroom a wax melt thing

since my search said women like those things .

Adding them to the cart, so I can check them out.

Not going to lie, I would be pissed as hell if I was the

delivery driver. I also do some quick searching and

look for simple cookie recipes. I wanted all of us to

decorate gingerbread men and sugar cookies. We

have everything for it. Sending all the recipes to my

phone.

Shutting my laptop down, I get up and make my way

to the shower, stripping my pants. I turn on the

shower and wait till it heats up before I step into the

shower. I hate that I was washing off my mate's scent

and cum off my body. I don't think we will be able to

stop fucking her. Scrubbing myself clean and my

hair, I grab the towel off the rack and dry off. I put

my pants in the laundry for the wash before walking

to my closet and putting on a new pair of sweatpants along with a shirt this time.

Walking into the kitchen, I start the coffee machine, looking outside and the clouds lighten up. Pulling my phone from my pocket, I open the saved recipe that I saved, and I start pulling out all the things we will need for cookies. I am half tempted to make the dough so that it is ready for her when she gets up from her sleep. Felix is the cook in the bonds, and when he is away I do the cooking. Who would want Kris in the kitchen? He works the appliance like he does a computer. He broke the microwave when he was cooking an easy meal. Now Frost can cook, but he says I am better with electric devices, so it's my duty when Felix is away. Frost and Kris can cook when they're with others, but alone, we would lose the house. I know I am taking a chance she might not even eat what I am going to cook but biscuits and gravy with bacon sound so good this morning. Who doesn't like biscuits and gravy? A criminal, that is who.

I finish placing the food on the island when I hear faint footsteps. Looking up, I see Emma coming from the hallway to the island. She is wearing the clothing that I brought into the bedroom last night. We agreed last night that we would dress her in her other mate's clothing since they are not her, so she can scent them even if she is only human. She has Felix's big t-shirt, Miles's sweatpants, and Leo's boxers. Her hair is a wild mess, looks like she has been fucked all night, and I mentally pat myself on the back. I watched her closely as she took the seat she was in yesterday. I noticed she is a creature by habit likes things a certain way that's okay. Keeping a close eye on her, I follow her movement as she without hesitation picks up the fork and digs in the food, taking a big bite. Her moans sent a chill down my back because she fills me with pride that she loves it. I heard that same moan while I was deep in her pussy.

Adjusting myself, I grab my plate and stand across from her while she eats.

Jasper: "If you are up to it, we could make some cookies and decorate them."

Emma:" I would love to make cookies with you. I want to thank you for cooking, it was fantastic."

Jasper:" I see that you feel safe with us now. Where are the other two at?"

Emma:" The other two are in the shower."

I watch as her cheeks flush red and she looks away. The girl might be shy now but when it comes to sex the girl is a piranha for some dick. If this is her nerves fucking, I can't wait till see feel at home.

A little while later the other two now sit at the island wolfing down their food. Kris has his hand on Emma's leg, and she smiles over at him. Frost has his chair angled in her direction. Both of them are enamored by her and I get it because I feel the same way about her.

Kris:"What are the plans for the day, do you want to watch TV or play games? We have the new UNO if you want to play that."

Frost:" Kris, have you not looked at your phone yet."

Kris:" No, but I will in a second. What is the plan for today?"

Jasper:" Well, we are going to make cookies and then maybe go play outside."

Kris:" Okay, well let me look at my phone, and then we will make cookies."

I watch as Kris gets up and places his plate in the sink before going over to the front door. I watch as he turns his phone on and waits till the dings start. I tap the island in front of Emma and point over to Kris. The dings started, and I saw him tap on his phone. I know when he enters the chat because my pocket vibrates, and then I watch as he reads the messages and I see when he sees the picture. His jaw tightens and the tips of his ears go red. He slowly turns to me and a flash of his wolf eye comes through. He takes a step and points out a finger.

Kris:" I can't believe you did that. Why would you send my dick in a group chat? It's like you want me to go and break all your toys. Keep pushing me, Jasper, and I will. I have been saying it for years, and I am not playing "you sent my dick in a group chat."

Emma: "Was it a good dick pic or a bad one."

Kris: "No, princess, it is a bad image of my dick ."

Ghosted Black Ice By D.Chaney

Emma: "Deflated boner pics are the worst."

She looks over at me and shackles her head. I see Kris type on his phone, and then my pocket vibrates.

Jasper:" I am just going to set up the live stream with the other guys so they can join us while we make cookies."

Frost:" I will do the dishes to get ready."

I walk out of the room to get the laptop, and I know that Frost is trying to give Emma and Kris a moment to calm down.

I look down at my phone and I see that Kris has changed his name in the group chat.

Felix has changed their name to muscledwolf

Kris has changed their name to bigdickwolf

Bigdickwolf-game on motherfucker, you just wait and see what I do back to you

witchdoc- I see that you have looked in the group chat

VampLeoDen-what a name Kris

Hornychef- This is funny as fuck, is Kris throwing a tantrum

GeekyWolf- he was about to, but I let Emma on him and said I was coming to get the laptop so we can live to stream with you three.

Honrychef- You left our mate with a mad Kris

Muscledwolf sent a photo

It was a picture of Emma sitting on Kris's lap with his hands on her back as she ran her hands down his face.

Ghosted Black Ice By D.Chaney

Muscledwolf- she has calmed him down a lot. You should hear all the sweet things he is saying to her.

Witchdoc-Her pussy has tamed the beast.

VampLeoDen- well if anyone could bring out that stubborn ass sensitive side it would have to be her

Hornychef- he has been closed off for so long I mean we know why I am just glad he has taken to her so well.

Witchdoc- well hurry up and set us up, want to see her

VampLeoDen- yep, we want to see her

Hornychef- yea hurry Jasper

Geekywolf- you are in for a surprise

Witchdoc- stop fucking out mate without us

I place my phone in my pocket and make my way

back downstairs.

## Chapter thirteen - cookies and snow angels

Emma

I never thought I would be in a kitchen with three men and three others on a video chat. I don't know if it was the cosmos or something else. When Jasper said we are going to make cookies today, I had to keep myself from jumping up and down. If I was not snowed in, I would be at home making cookies with my mom and Nana. Even though I am away from home, it feels like home. You would think that my family would freak out that I am not home, but I am a nutcase. Well, not a nut case out of a whim last year I decided to drive across the line and book a hotel room and stay for a week more likely that's what they think I am doing.

Baking cookies and the family vibe, the music, and the laughter. Kris has taken a seat on the island, he said he would be the judge of the cookies. Jasper and Frost are on either side of me. Frost has flour on his cheeks and nose. Jasper has the gingerbread man and woman, he has them on the island making kissing motions and the male on top of the female. We already had the sugar cookies done, and iced Felix was telling Jasper how to whisk and sift the flour to the point he said " that's it, no more Emma time till you learn to shut the hell up."

He turned the computer to the fireplace and gave me a wink, what the hell and are you kidding me? Jasper: " stop telling us how to make the cookies if you were here, then you can micromanage."

Ghosted Black Ice By D.Chaney

Felix: " It was my cousin's wedding, I offered to cook".

Kris:" that's why you are not home, and we are, so stop fucking complain."

Leo: " well all had things we had to do this time away. I had a client."

Miles:" I had a conference to attend. I can't help that."

Kris:" I say again it was your choice, and we are home with the lovely Emma so you three can shut the fuck up."

Miles, Felix, Leo: "Fuck you grump."

Ten minutes later, Kris turned the laptop back to us. I glanced at the laptop. All three of the men had their arms across their chests. If I didn't know they were grown men, I would think they were four year olds. I did try to keep the giggle inside, but it didn't happen. The giggle came out with a snort, and I braced myself on the island.

Emma: "The three of you look like four-year-olds who are pouting cause you three didn't get what they wanted."

Miles:" You think that's funny, don't you."

Emma:" Well, I think it's funny."

Leo:" you just wait."

Frost:" you can spank us all later."

I put the last cut cookie on the tray, I then move over to frost, who has icing in bags. That was a fun lesson to learn. I never thought I would have to learn how to pipe icing from a bag, but we all got to learn something someday . So frost and I iced the four dozen cookies. I am going to miss it when this ends. I got attached to the six of them and I love the cuddles. I might be sleep-deprived we fucked all night long, I think I fell asleep with a dick in my pussy. If I think about it too long, my clit will start throbbing again. There is just something about these men that makes me spend days in bed with them.

Frost

Frost: "If we are going to have some fun in the snow we need to get going." I state as I look over to Emma who is munching on a cookie. She has red icing on her nose. I was half tempted to lick it off.

Jasper: " Well let me go get you some gloves, hat, scarf, coat, and extra pair of socks." Jasper states that he walks out of the room to collect all the clothing our little mate will need.

Kris:" We need to do this quickly, they say another snow storm is going to hit in the next hour or so." He stands and moves to the fireplace to feed the fire.

I look down into Emma's eyes and run my now flour free hand down her cheek.
Frost: " Will you come outside and play with us and when we are done I will make you some hot chocolate loaded with marshmallows."

Ghosted Black Ice By D.Chaney

I watch as she blinks a few times and her breath hits

. Her arousal hits my nose stronger. My girl needs to

bend over this island and let me shove my cock in

her wet, tight little pussy. I lean down and run my

lips over her parted lips.

Frost: " After you eat some food, I will take you back

to bed and eat this pussy like one of those

gingerbread cookies you've been munching on."

I make chomping sounds with my mouth, and I lean

to the side and nibble at her neck.

I could bite her now and mark her as mine, it would

not take long for me to strip her pants to her knees.

Take her from behind as well, both cum I bite her

neck, locking my scent in her pussy and body.

Jasper: " hey you two, none of that will we get back inside the house". I pull from her neck and look up at Jasper and see he has his arms full. He gave me that serious look, he knew what I wanted to do, he could smell it on me. If I mark her as mine it would start a chain reaction, it would be one right after another fucking then marking her. The one thing that we all six promised we would wait on doing there was no mate marking till all six were in bed with her because it would drive the other bonded insane till they got to her.


Emma

I look ridiculous. I didn't see from the bundle in jasper arms how many clothing he truly had and more. I now have a big sweater on now along with a big coat. Two pairs of pants, they both have the drawstrings pulled to the max. Two pairs of thick wool socks in my feet. Jasper's hands were all over me, he even put the hat, scarf, gloves, even my shoes on my feet. I look like a marshmallow woman. I looked around and the frost and Kris were dressed and ready to go outside. I look over to see Jasper talking to the guys on the laptop.

Jasper: " miles, she is bundled up, stop already."
Jasper had his hands up in the air and looked back over to the three of us.
Jasper: " you know what, I am not doing this." I watch as he leans forward to the laptop and shuts

the lid. He pulls his hat on and starts making his way

to us..

Jasper: " Say bye Emma you will see them later." I

could help but say bye to a now shut laptop.


Jasper: " will video chat them again later."

I feel Jasper's hand on my back as he nudges me to

the front door.  Stepping down the steps to the snow.

I hear a ding, like it's one of those camera doorbells

being alerted. I don't know if it's the weight of all

the clothing. I let out a squeal as I tumbled over and

landed on my back in the snow. All I could do was

laugh. The snow storms have turned the sky gray. I

close my eyes and take at the moment, my mind

sounds like a broken record.  That these men are

mine and it's okay to have them. Deep down inside, I

Ghosted Black Ice By D.Chaney

am scared that I will embrace this with the guys, and it was all a game, and they use me. I feel the hand grab mine on each side.

Emma: "Thank you for this moment. I appreciate it." Nothing really needed to be said or done; we were just taking it all in.

I might have taken a nap in the snow. It was when I felt little ice drips hit my face, opening my eyes. I look up and see that a new snow storm has arrived, big fluffy puffs coming down from the sky. I stick my tongue out, trying to catch the snow.
Leo: "Are you eating snow, pretty girl".
I let go of the guy's hands and leaned forward, glanced around, and remembered the ding when I

was going down the steps. I see the little camera on the door and give it a wink and stick my tongue out all the way to catch the puffs.

Jasper: " Hey fuck faces, this is our time." he says, leaning up besides me.

Miles: "You have had plenty of time."

I am looking at the camera when all of a sudden a snow ball has hit the camera. I look to see Kris standing with snow covered hands.

Miles: "hey, that's fucking rude."

Jasper: "Rude will be me turning off the Wi-Fi so we can have some fun. Now get off the camera."

I feel something hit my back, turning back to Kris. I see Kris with a smirk on his face, and he has another snowball ready to launch. I dodge over frost and the snowball misses me. I lean down and whisper in Frost's ear.

Emma:" Help me beat him with snowballs."

Frost leans up and kisses me on the cheek before he rolls over and gets on his knees, he automatically starts packing snow into balls. I get to my knees and do the same. I get a snowball to the chest I counter by throwing one to his face, I miss and hit him on the shoulder.  I don't know how long we played. We ended up in the woods throwing and dodging snowballs.


Emma


We stumbled into the house where snow is caked in places I never knew snow could be caked. I started to take off my snow covered clothing when my hand was slapped away and Kris was standing in front of me. I lean toward him and lift up my arms so he can take off my sweater. Another set of hands takes my hat, and it's taken off along with the scarf. When the second layer is off me, I am picked up and placed on the island. Frost is making, going around the kitchen and pulling out a pop and milk and chocolate and a container filled with mini marshmallows. I look for the other two, and I see Kris placing wood in the fireplace. Jasper has disappeared and the clothing that was on the rug now gone.

It was not long before there was steamy hot chocolate placed into my hands. The warmth from the cup seeps into my skin, warming me up. The laptop is open, and the other three males are talking about their hotel rooms and how the food sucks. Miles talks about watching missing work in the ER and how he has been watching new emergency techniques. Felix says he's been working on a few new recipes as well since he had some downtime and can't wait for me to try them. Leo sits with his pasture as straight as a board. He just says that he's been working on some clients' cases.

The more we talk, the more I fall, and I am falling hard. We sit at the island with the three others at the head of the table. The three have ordered food as well. Miles looks to be eating a salad and Leo looks to be eating a steak with baked potatoes. Felix the chef, the pain in the butt, shocked me the most when he was eating pizza.

Jasper made grilled cheese and tomato soup so good and perfect after a while in the snow. The guys each took turns on asking me questions. I don't question their kindness but I am wary of it and hate that I feel this way. When the meals were all eaten I looked over to frost and he made a bite motion with his mouth and I was thrown over my shoulder and rushed through the halls of the house. When I am thrown on a bed I lean up and see the three men and the other on the laptop all looking at me with hungry eyes.

Frost: " All six of us are going to have fun tonight." He moves in front of me and strips the sweatpants off of me. The pants are thrown on one of the chairs by the fireplace, Frost steps away from me and moves around the bed to climb in behind me.

Ghosted Black Ice By D.Chaney

Frost: " Now spread their legs as far apart as you can."

I move them as far as I can to the point that there is a faint pain in my hip. Frost moves my hair to the side and sucks the side of my neck, causing me to moan. I didn't even know when Kris came to the side of the bed and, Well, hovered over my legs.

Jasper:" Well, princess, we decided to show the three home always what they're missing."

I watch as he brings the laptop toward the bed and lays it down on the bed. You could see my pussy and the tips of my breast. Jasper goes to the other side of my bed from Kris . He hovers a leg and then he and Kris sit gently on my legs, locking them in place. Frost is still working on my neck and now rubbing my breast. I could not help but moan out in pleasure.

I was wrong. What Kris and Jasper did next took me to the next level. Kris and Jasper both run their fingers over my pussy lips.

Miles: " Open them pussy lips, let me see her clit."

Without hesitation, they both grab pussy lips and pull them open. The air hits my clit and I can feel myself getting wet by the second.

Felix: "Kris, move your fingers around her clit."

Kris does what he is told, and he moves his hand around my clit. I could do nothing and to be honest I don't want to do anything, so I moan and let out little pants.

Miles: " Pinch her nipples, Frost."

Frost also follows what he is told to do. What have I gotten into the amount of pleasure?

Leo: "Jasper, put two fingers in her pussy hole, let me watch as her skin tries to swallow your fingers." I feel Jasper's thumb run down to my pussy till he reaches my entrance and pushes his finger into me. My pussy tightens around his fingers, causing my body tingles.

Leo: " That's it, tighten around his fingers, milk his fingers."

Miles: " Are you going to cum little mate. Are you going to let your juice cover all over my bed."

Leo: " Add another finger, jasper, and spread her more ."

Jasper adds a finger now. I have three moving back and forth out of me. My muscles are clenched around his fingers. I can feel the built-up pressure deep inside. I tried to close my legs, but Kris and jasper body held me in place. Frost moves his hand from my breast, close to Kris. When Kris bit down on my nipple, I came undone and was held in place as my body shakes all over. Moans and shouts ring out with mine. I realize my three watchers haven been playing with their cocks. With the sound of their own realize I am again cumming undone on what can I say I am a cum cummer. I have a thing with men who cum and cum loud and proud.

My body was jello and I don't know how many times I have cummed. I know my jaw hurts, and I have cum leaking out of my pussy, I have cum painted on my neck down to my stomach. My pussy is sore, but again she wants more. Later, I am going to need a

Ghosted Black Ice By D.Chaney

talk with my pussy. She is acting all out of shorts. I can wait to try to have two of them at the same time in my pussy. Not for a little while thought because my pussy is sore as fuck, three of the men I have fallen for had watched me get fucked eaten and me suck cock. I would hate to be the person who cleans their room and sees all the stains they created. I remember one of the guys coming into the room with a washcloth and cleaning me up well. The best they could with a few rounds of cum, it would take a soak in the tub to let it all wash away.

I hear the crackling of the fireplace crack and pop across the room. I look to the window that is facing the front of the house. I see the snow storm has arrived more than before, and you can't even see the woods that surround the house. I lay there in Kris' arms as he squeezed me tighter. I watched as the snow came down. I need to come to reality and realize that this was just a few days of passion and when the time comes this will all be a dream. We all will have to go back into the real world. This cabin in the woods has been more than a safe haven. I think we all could be something, but my mind knows better.

I want this more than anything. I want them all. I want to spend the rest of my life with these men. I could see the halls in this house filled with kids and laughter. I can see photos filling the walls with us and are family members. I want it and I can see it but know deep down that it all will come to an end. I guess Nana was right. I would be getting several

dicks.

Chapter Fourteen -A Day In Bed  (Day Two)

Kris

Emma is spread out on me, her nose is buried in my neck, taking my scent in. Her breath tickles my neck with each breath she takes in and out, her lips grazing my neck. She was worn out, and I love that she is ours. She takes us all in stride. She takes my grumpiness in and shows me compassion and love. He handles Jasper's hyper off-the-wall things, he does not like to talk about his ADHD so we don't mention it. If he wanted her to know, he would have to be the one to tell her. Then we have Frost who is like a combination of both of us, the more she is around us the more she changes us. I don't know if she believes us when we tell her she is the one for us and that we want her forever. I see the pain in her eye and the second of hesitation in her eye. No amount of us doing and trying to show her that we love and want her. She has to see it on her own to realize we are not going anywhere. If she leaves us, we will find her and show her the love she never knew that she needed. If she keeps running, we will find her every time or follow.

So I pull her closer to me and kiss the top of her head. I know the storms will let up soon, and then I don't know what will happen. I just know that we can't lose her. We just found her after waiting so long for her. It would kill all of us if she walked away from us, but we all will follow and find her. I look over to the big windows and watch as the snow falls. I hope the snow storms last for the next million years because no amount of time will be good enough with her.

Jasper

I snuggle into Emma back. I feel her chest move up and down and move her ass across my cock. If my dick didn't feel like it was going to fall off, I would be deep in her pussy while she is snuggling into Kris. We have been fucking in waves since she asks to take a bath or shower, I don't really know. I know the guys are also tired. She is our sex-crazed princess. I think about all the time we have been spending and like the others I can feel it, we can't let her walk away she is ours even if she doesn't

know the truth yet. I kiss her back and snuggle
deeper into her.


Frost

I am not ashamed to admit I was cuddled into
Jasper. I have been lying here awake while the
others sleep. Well, when they finally fell asleep, I
listened to them. The three of them breathed slowly
to a slumber. I don't know why, but I know she is
going to run from us, and I can help but feel the
pain lingering in my body. It has not even happened
yet, but I know in my heart and so does my body. I
hope I am wrong about it, and she doesn't leave. If
she does leave, she takes us with her so we can be in
her life, but time will tell. As long as the storm is
here, she will stay with us. We all would love to

spend time getting to know her family cause soon she will have tons of in-laws, five mother in laws and eighteen father in laws. We have not told the parents yet, but when we do this house will be bursting at the seams. Let the spirits help us; they will spoil their little mate.

Emma

We ended up sleeping in the bed till late that afternoon. I was just too tired to get up from the bed, and I really didn't want to. For the first time that I woke up in this cabin with these men, Frost is the one cooking. He heated up cans of chicken and noodle soup for all of us. Frost brought a tray of bowls into the bedroom. I made the decision to get up and take a shower. The problem was, I had three others join me in the shower. The shower was big; it had multiple shower heads, eight to be honest. There is a seating ledge under the shower heads, Jasper turns on one of the shower heads as Kris keeps me in his arms as he waits till the water is warm. Frost went into the bathroom I used the other day that has the essential oils wash I liked too much. So Kris and I wait, with me in his arms.

Kris walks me into the shower.  I am soon met with warm water meeting my hair, water cascades down my nipples getting excited as they always do when I am taking a bath or shower.

Emma: " I can stand, you know."

I say into the air so maybe one of them will realize I do have legs and I can also use them. I am met with a slap on the ass and a Kris cock thrust into my pussy lips rubbing on my clit.

Kris: " You do, but I like to keep you in my arms."

Emma: "asshole!"

Kris continues to rub his cock on my clit which causes me to lean my head back letting the water wash over my face and down are bodies and I can hear the slapping of skin . Frost comes into the close and pours some essential oil shampoo into his hand and works it into a lather in my hair. He moves his fingers into my hair, giving my scalps a massage. I feel something rub against my legs that are wrapped around Kris. Jasper has a puff sponge and rubs it along my legs and feet .

Jasper: " Flip her around, Kris, so I can clean her pussy."
Kris lets me down on the tiled floor before turning me around and picking me back up. He sits down on the ledge with me still on his lap. I think Jasper is about to take a washcloth and clean me, but I was so wrong. Jasper picks my legs and places them to hang over Kris legs. I watch as Frost detaches the shower head from the wall and switches the setting pulse. Frost hands the shower head over to Jasper, who is smirking. No way was he going to use a shower head to clean me. I look down between my

legs as Jasper with one hand opens my up and rubs his knuckle over my clit.

Jasper: " you ready baby ."

I shake my head yes and take a deep breath as the shower head moves over my pussy lips to my clit. The vibrations on my already sensitive clit, I could not help when my body started to shake, and I cum over and over. Jasper moves the shower head to my pussy hole and lets the shower head push water into my hole. The water whooshing in and out of me turns me on more. Kris is rubbing his cock into my ass crack, rubbing it in and out my checks. Leaning my head back into Kris, I'm moaning out he takes a hand and wraps it around my neck. He tightens his hold on my neck and whispers in my ear.

Kris: " Is my little princess dick hungry would you like me to push my dick into this pussy and fuck you until you scream."

Emma: " Yes please."

Before I can think or move Jasper has moved back and Kris has me above his cock, his hand back around my neck squeezing, cutting off some of my sir supply. I go to reach up and claw at his hand when he slams his cock into me. I move up and down and feel jasper move the shower head across my back, letting the water pound into my back. I was still shocked when I felt someone spread my ass cheek and I felt the shower head hit my puckered hole. He pulls the shower head away from me and I hear the shower head change settings. When the shower head met by ass again, it was not thumping like before but a solid stream. Jasper has it pointed right at my butt hole. The pleasure of both has me biting into Kris' shoulder as I keep moving my hips and she shower head following me and tightens my pussy around Kris' cock. I hear him grunt and thrust up into me. I am worn out and I can't move.

I woke up in the living room. I look out the window and see the snow still continues to come down, but instead of the puff balls it's a powder. I look down, and I see that I am in an oversized shirt and a pair of boxers. The fireplace was lit and above it the news was on in big bold letters the roads will be back open on Christmas Eve. There is only one thing I need to do. I need to get home before Christmas or Nana will have my ass and be very mad at me. Christmas is her holiday, and she is always the first one up and the first one to be at the presents. I also have to be home to make our dip a family tradition. I could take them with me, but I won't let this be a snowstorm romance.

Jasper is in the kitchen again cooking, I even know at this point. Kris was beside me watching the news. Frost was punching a dummy he hit in the chest and would kick it in the head and give all kinds of movements. At peace, that is what is happening, Jasper comes before me and places a plate of cookies in front of me.

Jasper:" Eat baby, you have to be hungry."

With that, he walks back into the kitchen. I pick up a cookie and place it into Kris' mouth so he can have a bite. He eats, takes a bite and chews. I watch as his throat moves as he swallows, why the fuck in this man so addiction.

 Emma: "Can we sleep down here tonight? I want to watch movies with you."

Ghosted Black Ice By D.Chaney

Frost stops punching the dummy and turns around facing us. Stepping closer to where I am laying.

Jasper, Kris, Frost: "Of course if that is what you want." The three of them say in unison, Frost sits down on the couch now watching the news.

I snuggle deeper into the blanket that was draped over Kris and I and we snuggle as he continues to watch the news with Kris. Who knew Kris was a big snuggle bug, the moody motherfucker loves the cuddles, he almost demands them. Who am I to tell my big guy no when he gives me these puppies mother fucking eyes that make my pussy want to ride his dick again. No bad pussy, no cuddles with dicks, no dick.

Emma

It was hours later, and we all decided to play UNO. The only catch is we play it my way and since Nana knows me so well she had packed several boxes in my survival bag. Putting them all together and handing out twenty cards to each. Took the guys a bit to catch on, but they loved it in the end. We played several rounds and ate some snacks. Whoever won, I would get on their lap and make out with them.

It was a good break for my pussy. Well, sorta, she wants more and more of them. Jasper made dinner and instead of eating at the island we are sitting on the couch. Kris beside me and Jasper on the other side, Frost sat in the corner of the lounge by my knee. We talked for hours, and they asked me all sorts of questions.

What were my favorite movies?

What books do I like to read?

Favorite Candy?

When was my birthday?

Summer or winter?

What toppings do I like on pizza?

What is my favorite sub sandwich?

My comfort foods?

Favorite flower?

Only because I know I would be shamed if I didn't when they ask me about my favorite flower. I don't even think it is a flower but it's a family joke that nana plays on everyone even in public. So I yell pussy and in a lower tone willow. The three looked at me like I lost my damn mind  and I busted out laughing.  Then they started laughing with me. I couldn't help but be grateful that they have a great sense of humor.

Emma: " I love lavender because of the smell and the fact it's purple and the calming effect it has."

The questions lasted a little while longer before I got sleepy again, they wore me out. I fight it as long as I can and snuggle into a warm body and blanket.

Ghosted Black Ice By D.Chaney

Chapter Fifteen-Final Day And Making A Plan

(Last Day)

Miles

I feel through the bond that something's not right. I have been working on getting a flight home like my two other bonded brothers. Something bad was about to happen and I couldn't stop it. I tried to call Kris and the others and tell him I think they need to watch our mate, but I was unable to get a hold of them. After the night when we all watched are mate get fucked and fingered, I knew she would be tired, and it might take a few days.

So not answering is not a big deal, but I need to warn them. I send a message in a group text that still has been unseen on their end. I have been ordering plants for her bathroom that will thrive, along with some essential oils for her baths.

I open up my laptop and start a live chat with the other two. Leo pops on the screen first he is shirtless and what looks like in bed.

Miles:" Have you heard anything from home."

Mid-sentence, Felix pops on the screen and looks like he just got out of the shower.

The both of them shake their heads no and say nothing.

Felix: "Should we be worried that they're not answering the phone."

Miles: "Yes, no, well I don't really know I am worried I have this feeling that something is going to happen.

Ghosted Black Ice By D.Chaney

All I could hope is that it has nothing to do with our mate.

Leo:" I mean, it could be because she is tired, we all had a long night. She was getting so much dick that they all passed out."

Miles:" Have you heard that the airport will be reopening tomorrow? They have been working nonstop. I have been watching their social media, and they have been having plow trucks and deicers." My body was vibrating with need. I needed to get home to my girl and wrap myself around her to let her aura meet mine. The need to make sure she is healthy and fine burns my body. I've been leaving flowers everywhere when I have this urge. Roses I have been piling them up for days, red potent our love is strong even when we are all not mated.

My phone vibrated in my hand. I almost declined when I thought the airport could be calling. Clicking the call over, not saying a word to the boys.

Leo

Mile's screen goes blank like he took a call.

Felix: "hold on a second, let me get some clothing on." his screen on the feed has gone blank like miles.

For the past few days, I can't stop from letting my teeth extend from my gums. I am not hungry, the cooler blood has sated my need for food. What I required was my mate, I needed to mark her as mine and we both are blood. The red haze has come over my eyes a lot these last few days, talking to her and getting to know her and who she is as a person. The way her brown eyes are so deep in the darker side that they're almost black. The way she bites her lip as she talks, and she feels flustered.

The last we have been to hell and I know Miles and Felix are feeling like I am, there is nothing worse than losing the first few days of bonding with their mate. Just the thought of this has my teeth trying to pop out. Besides that, I've been ordering things for her room to keep my mind busy. I've been on all these sites. I even hired a custom rug maker to do a moon and stars rug. I found the perfect bedding that matches the dark blue and star hues. I found these black out curtains that have stars cut out of them, so the room would be dark, and the sun will show in through the stairs to look like the night sky. I found tons of pillows. After all the found books I bought her romances, zodiac, astrology, and art.

I was about to open up the shopping app again when miles popped on the screen again. With a smile, it looked like it would fall off his face and land on the floor.

Before I could ask what the hell is going on, Felix comes back on the screen with the same look. At least he was dressed this time.

Miles:" the airport has just called and said that I should be there in the morning and I should be home sometime before noon."I watch as his eyes turn a hint of green and flowers pop out through his clasp hands.

Felix: "I got the same call. I have a ride home sometime in the morning. I am thinking about going ahead and moving to the airport and just wait till my flight is ready." I see miles shake his head in agreement

Deep down in myself, I was jealous of the two of them getting a way home and getting the call we all have been waiting to get. The hint of anger came through my bones and settled in my heart. I never should have taken my client case. I listen to them talk about what they will do when they get there,

stopping at the local donut shop and getting our

mate some food along with our brothers.

I don't know if I was chasing those dreams, or I was

just in the fog. I almost missed the call on the

screen, some number I don't know. I break off the

live call and answer the incoming one.

Leo- Hello

Caller-Am I'm speaking with Mr. Thorne

The voice on the line sounds like an old lady that

smokes forty packs of cigarettes a day and sounds

like she has not had dick ever.

Leo-Yes, this is he

Ghosted Black Ice By D.Chaney

Caller-well, I am calling to tell you that your standby flight leaves at two am.

Leo-Thank you for calling

My phone bounces back to the live feed with the other. I know that I had the same wicked grin as well, and I could not help but blurt out and break the conversation.

Leo: " I guess I am going to have to pack as well. I got the call that my flight leaves early in the morning."

I could not help but let my teeth pop out of my gums. My emotions could not help it. We will be with our mate soon. Me and the guys spoke for a while before we all decided to pack up and head to the airport. By this time in the morning I will be in front of my mate and we'll be telling her all about

the mate and what we are.


Felix


I have been so horny lately, and I just realized how

that sounds in my head. Well it, not a lie, my

demonic horns have been out. The need for my

mate is getting stronger and stronger. I even texted

Jasper to tell him to save all the clothing she has

worn in a separate laundry basket. Not to wash

them because I wanted to roll around in them, I

want to lick the boxer she has used. Lick where her

pussy meets the cloth and her little juices leak out. I

wanted them because I had to warm up to her to be

with her as a human, so meeting a demonic mate is harder than one will think seeing a man with a horn is not an everyday thing. Then again it might be different, all I know is I want her clothing by her, so I can roll and lick clean. I am going to look like a full on ass cat, my chest is rumbling as I growl out.

I pack up all my things and look in the mirror and see my horns flare alongside my head. Good thing humans could not see supernatural things unless it was a mate thing. Human mates can see all their flaws and more. Good thing it is the winter, so hats are a thing so when I get home so as not to freak out. Emma I will have my horns covered, and we can ease her into who we all are, one of us being a demon and Leo a vampire and Miles a witch and finally the three wolf boys.

Here we all are all around the United States in three separate airports. All waiting to get home to start their life with their mate. To show her their life and what they can provide for her. Introduce her to their family. For us to meet her family and show them we can love her.

Chapter Sixteen - Silent Like A Ghost

Emma

Kris and I fell asleep together, I woke up laying on top of Kris, my stomach on his stomach and his arms wrapped around my back. I can't imagine what I looked like on top of him. I had a dream of three wolves surrounding me in the woods while three figures stood over us. There was not an ounce of fear in the dream, I felt like I was home, being among the wolves and the men. I felt like I found my peace and where I truly belong and the chance of everything I snuggled deeper into Kris' body listening to my surroundings when I was awake earlier Jasper was cooking food and Frost was using the dummy being punched. I thought he would for sure have gone back to hitting the dummy. The room was silent, the clinking from the kitchen and the sound of slapping from Frost was gone.

Opening my eyes, I pull my face from Kris's neck, putting pressure on my knees that are beside both Kris's hips. Kris' hand goes limp to his sides. I am pushing myself up so that I am hovering above him as silently as I can be. I try, and I mean the word try to cause as soon as I lift my leg to swing over Kris. His hands grab my hips and pull me closer, rubbing his cock against my needy pussy.

Kris: "Where do you think you're going, princess."

He still has his eyes closed when he nips at my lips.

Ghosted Black Ice By D.Chaney

I look at him, and I mean I look at him. Since waking up in the cabin, I have not felt a sense of calm till now. I continued to thrust his cock against the borrowed boxers. Kris pulls a hand away from my hip and grabs my boob, giving it a squeeze, I shift and start rubbing myself on his cock. I feel his hand move from my breast down my belly to my covered pussy. He rubs a knuckle over my covered pussy lips, putting pressure down as he feels my clit. Circling my clit with his knuckle, I can feel the boxers getting wet. I let out a wine as he abandoned my clit and moved down to my thigh, slipping his fingers through the bottom of the boxers. I feel his finger spider crawl up to my soaked entrance. Breathing heavily I move my hips to feel him more moving my lips over his I circle my arms around his neck. One finger two fingers and the feel of his hard cock, the little nibbles have me moaning in his mouth. Breathing deep, I feel Kris take his finger from my pussy and stick them in his mouth and suck my juices off his fingers. I watch as he throws his head back and moans, his hips move until they settle on the couch. I feel a wet spot on my butt. Looking down at his crotch, I see a wet stain, the proof that he came with me. I jerk his hand from his mouth and stick those fingers in mine, sucking and licking them clean.

Kris: "You're my dirty girl, aren't you?"

Popping his finger from my mouth, I suck him and my juices off his fingers. He pulls his fingers from my mouth before placing his lips on mine.

Ghosted Black Ice By D.Chaney

Kris flattens me and stands up. I tighten my legs around his waist. He moved us through the living room to the kitchen, placing me on the island. It's like I am the sun and. The guys are the planets. I was swarmed by them. Frost and Jasper appear out of thin air.

Kris: "I will be right back."

He leans down, kisses my forehead and walks off down the hallway.

Jasper: "I made meatloaf and mashed potatoes for dinner."

He comes up beside me and has a fork full of food in front of my mouth. How the fuck did he get a plate full that fast. Taking a bite, I chew. I watch Frost come up with his plate and feed me a fork full of mashed potatoes. They are both on either side feeding me, Kris comes back in short and no shirt, so mouth-watering. Kris steps up and holds a drink to my lips. I take it I won't be getting my plate, the three will be feeding. Spoon after spoon and a little time later I am being carried to the couch again, this time I am lying on top of Jasper. The fireplace gives a romantic vibe, the pop and flick of the fire give the room an orange and yellow hue. Perfect for watching Christmas movies, and that's what we do.

Ghosted Black Ice By D.Chaney

Frost sits beside Jasper and Kris sits on the other side. Frost and Kris have their hands on my hips, Jasper wraps his arms around me, and I lean back, putting my head on his shoulder. The four of us spent thirty minutes bickering about whether Die Hard is a Christmas movie or not. Kris states that just because a movie is during Christmas doesn't mean it is a Christmas movie.

Emma: "That's exactly why it's a Christmas movie. This is like saying Halloween is not a Halloween movie."

Kris: " You all are nuts, it's just an action movie."

Emma: " I'm starting to regret letting you play with my pussy. Keep talking to the big guy and this pussy will ghost you."

I look away from him and cross my arms, focusing

back on the TV.rms,. Jasper hands runs up and

down my stomach, and he kisses my shoulder and

neck. Kris and Frost have trailed the hands from my

hips to my thighs. Squeezing here and there and

nudging me for kisses and I give them what they

want.


We watched three of the Die Hard. After a while I

looked around and Kris and Frost were asleep,

letting out faint snores. Jasper's arms have already

fallen to his sides as he is asleep. I lay there

watching the fire that is slowly dying out. I don't

know why, but I made the choice. Self-doubt and

being scared of relationships and the fact I let my

head run rampant with thought that I shouldn't in

the end the fear wins. I slowly and stealthily as I can while listening to their breathing, I get off Jasper. I creep away and through the house, grab my stuff, not caring about the UNO cards we opened up earlier. I hope when they play, they remember me. Silent as ever, I slip my shoes on. I turn back to the three men on the couch, they look of peace and happiness, and I know I already feel the pain in my chest as I turn around and step to the door. Unlocking the door and slipping out, making it to my car. I unlock the driver's door, and throw my stuff in the seat. Closing my door as silent as I can. I sent up to the universe to please let my car start, or I will have to figure something else out. I have never been happier when the universe gave me one up and my front and back windshield were clear of snow. I turned the key to start my car without a hitch. She was silent like the night. Keeping my headlights off. I pull out of their driveway to a road that leads me back to the main road I hope, looking around I know where I am and where I need to avoid in the near future. I would not be able to drive by this place everyday knowing they are there and what we shared. But I am a realist, and there was no way I could have all six men in my life. This will most likely be the biggest mistake of my life. I don't have time for relationships. I travel all the time for photography jobs. I could not give up my passion because I want to be dicked down by six men all the time.

Turning right toward the road that leads me to my home, I couldn't help but cry as I left, the best thing that had ever happened to me. There is no way I can be in a relationship with six men. I don't know why my heart and body ache. All my body and mind wants to do is turn around and go back to them. I don't think so. I tell myself I can't keep living in a fantasy. I keep heading home. Make it a little ways before I look back one last time. Looking in the rearview mirror to the place I pulled out of, and I see a car turn on the road that leads to my dream. To the men I abandoned, to the men I have officially ghosted. They were my Black Ice. I didn't see them till it happened, and there was nothing I could do about it. I did the only thing I knew and ran.

## A Little Bit More

As I drive, I look to the right side of the road and in an open field that usually grows corn in the summer now snowed over. That deer from days ago is there, running back to where I came from. I should have gone back, I should have never left.

If I was not so hyped up and in my head, I would have gone back and climbed back on the couch onto Jasper and let him wrap his arms around me. Wake up to the four of us in the kitchen eating. I snuggle with my grumpy Kris as he kisses my head.

I also know I couldn't miss Christmas, nothing like being on Nana's shit list if you are not present on Christmas, and she lets you know it is the cold shoulder. She won't speak to you and when you try to talk to her, she turns away. So I had to get home for Christmas, so I am not in Nana shit house. I have a traditional drip to make and make up for missing the stocking opening.

Dad won't give a fuck he is like that he just lets you be as long as it's not drugs or illegal activities, he is pretty laid back. Mom, well she was a worrier she would have been up all night and Dad would have told her on repeat that I am an adult and will be home when I am home.

Ghosted Black Ice By D.Chaney

A million and ten thoughts run through my head as I keep driving.

To be continued in part two

*"Thanks for flicking the pages, I knew you would."*

*... D. Chaney*

Coming In The New Year

*(Part Two)*

COMING SOON

Part Two Of The Pussy Willow Series

Ghosted Black Ice By D.Chaney

Make sure to follow me:

Thank you for reading and I hope you enjoyed

The Pussy Willow Series

The fun fact is nothing more embarrassing than your Nana asking you if you knew what her favorite plant was and her yelling pussy real loud and willow low. Yep, in public and all...